Crossing Neal

A NOVEL

Catina Noble

crowecreations.ca

Crossing Neal © 2025 Catina Noble
First Crowe Creations Print Publication November 2025

Cover from iStock. Credit: zabelin ID:1425466413 (Location: Ukraine, Park Ranger)
Cover Design © 2025 Crowe Creations
Interior design by Crowe Creations
Text set in Times New Roman; headings set in Staccato
Author photo by David Villeneuve

Crowe Creations ISBN: 978-1-998831-42-5

ONTARIO ARTS COUNCIL
CONSEIL DES ARTS DE L'ONTARIO

an Ontario government agency
un organisme du gouvernement de l'Ontario

I would like to thank the Ontario Arts Council
for awarding me the grant that allowed me
the time to write this project.

Dedicated to Phyllis Bohonis and Sherrill Wark. These two extraordinary women and authors have been the shining light, not only in my writing life, but in my ordinary one as well.

There's always a way out.

Year 2065

1

During the last Agency meeting, it was decided that crosses, the people who lived within the City of Kneel, had too much freedom. Too much of anything was never good—especially in a case where freedom was a concern. This was becoming an issue.

Hundreds of people, all of whom lived inside a city with a twenty-yard-high cement wall that surrounded the entire area, were called crosses, and they were governed and kept in place by The Agency. The Agency was an elected body consisting of thirteen male members including Captain Neal who controlled most of the power. Well, all of it, actually. Captain Neal had been Vice-Captain until the previous Captain had mysteriously died in his sleep.

Having thirteen Agents provided extra insurance in case of a tie vote. Usually Captain Neal tipped it in his favor—one of the many perks that came with the job. One that he thoroughly enjoyed. The Captain was a formidable and handsome man. He stood a towering six foot four and weighed approximately two hundred and twenty-five pounds. He was always dressed impeccably. His attire always consisted of black dress pants and solid black T-shirts that were well-suited to his jet-black hair. His hairstyle was an unvarying buzz cut achieved with a size two razor every six weeks on the dot. A person could get lost in his mesmerizing emerald green eyes.

The fewer people with freedom and power, the better. Things ran more smoothly that way. Being controlled benefited everyone and maintained the city's well-being. Recently, things had been getting out of hand. This wasn't good. The audacity of the crosses deliberately disobeying orders had to be stopped, no matter the cost. If rules were being broken, it would inevitably create a domino effect and lead to complete chaos. The Captain would not let this happen. If it continued, it would be only a matter of time before The Agency would be overthrown, possibly each member killed. Maybe Captain Neal was overthinking matters but that was his job. He had to think of worst case scenarios. There was no way he could take any chances. In his city, he needed to be assured the people knelt to his power.

What was to happen now was not The Captain's fault. The blame lay completely with the crosses. If they hadn't been pushing so hard against what he believed was best for everyone, he wouldn't be in this position now. The Agency had implemented harsher rules assisted by the added eyes from drones. He had at least a dozen large drones flying all over the city which gave him access to information at all times. This helped keep most crosses in line. It had to be done; there had been little choice. In The Captain's experience, anything deemed necessary was best applied sooner than later. Of course everyone had rights, but there were limits to absolutely everything. This did not apply to him, but did apply to the other members of The Agency and, of course, to all crosses within his city.

❊ ❊ ❊

The Captain rose, arms folded dominantly across his chest, and made the crowd keep silent for a full five minutes before he addressed them. He thought it best to keep everyone on their toes. The crosses needed to know he was in charge right from the beginning.

"You must all learn to trust The Agency—as a whole and individually. We have only your best interests and safety at heart. Take a moment and look around. Times are changing. Things are not as they used to be. Survival is of the utmost importance and if we are to make this happen, we must work together. It's not difficult. If everyone follows the rules we will get along just fine. The rules must be obeyed." The Captain paused and looked up as a drone flew past him.

His eyes searched the crowd. Adult crosses of various ages were lined up in front of him, listening to his every word. His city, Kneel, consisted of twelve blocks. Each city block contained fifty units. All Agency members had been assigned several blocks and were responsible for whatever happened inside them.

Tonight's gathering had been initiated to inform everyone of the tagging procedure, the accompanying rules, and making sure everyone in the city was chipped. Everyone contained in The Cell had already been done. This was, logically, the next step for everyone else.

The Captain continued. "Each of you will receive a chip. It will not hurt. It will feel like a quick pin prick. It will be administered into your pinky. You can choose which hand."

He paused, pulled out a black device from his pocket that was nearly two inches smaller than the height and width of a pen.

"Don't mess with the chip. You won't even feel it once it's there. If you are found trying to manipulate the chip in any way, you will be given a strike. The first strike will land you three months in The Cell. A second strike will land you six months in The Cell. The third strike will be the final one because if you are caught, there won't be anything more to talk about. I'll leave it at that."

At this point, The Captain deliberately stopped talking to scan the crowd again. He wanted to see the fear in their eyes. This would be a testament to his leadership. If the crosses feared him, they would obey and respect him.

"We are not heartless. There'll be accidental incidents, of course, and we expect that. These things happen. Adjusting to new things takes time. We know that. For example, someone might accidentally cut their baby finger, the one with the chip. It could happen. In that case, kindly report it to a member of The Agency immediately. It's important you don't wait because from the moment the chip has been tampered with, you will have only one chance to report it and receive another chip. If you choose not to report the tampered with or missing chip, well... That's your choice. However. Note. If we find out, it's an automatic strike against you."

The crowd remained silent.

"Now. Once you've been tagged with a chip by an Agent, you may go home. Thank you for your patience and understanding."

2

Scotia stretched as tall as possible to see over the city square. She was two or three rows back in a group of people. It took a moment but she spotted Brie, her older sister, among the crowd waiting to be tagged.

She couldn't help but worry about Brie. Scotia spoke her mind sometimes, but usually had the good sense to think twice before letting the words out. The same couldn't be said for Brie. If something came to Brie's mind, she blurted it out. There was no holding back. Scotia hoped there wouldn't be a fuss with the tagging. If her sister was smart, she would be tagged like everyone else and if necessary, complain about it privately later. If Brie said the wrong thing to The Agency, it would likely land her in The Cell. Scotia shivered, not from the cold, but from the fear she felt for her sister's safety.

She wished she were with her sister now, holding hands. Maybe some courage would rub off on her. Being thrown into The Cell wouldn't be worth a few ill-chosen words. *After all, it was nothing but a stupid chip.*

All the crosses were frightened, but no one knew what to say or do. Perhaps they hoped, like Scotia, that this was a nightmare, that soon they would wake up and laugh about sharing the same dream.

She was uneasy. Somehow, deep inside, Scotia knew this wasn't the end of The Agency's new rules. It was the beginning. People were already whispering. There had to be more to the chips besides identifying which block you were from, your personal health stats, or where you were at any given time. It seemed like way too much work to be that simple. No one knew what the chips were really for—and that was the scariest part of all.

Ted touched Scotia's shoulder. She turned around, and when she saw who it was, her smile instantly disappeared. "I wonder why they're really doing this to us. It's not right. The Agency doesn't own us."

"Keep your voice down," Ted replied, looking around. "You don't want them to hear you." His eyes pleaded with hers.

❀ ❀ ❀

Captain Neal grasped Scotia's left wrist. "This will only take a second. Left or right hand, just leave it and there won't be a problem. Simple."

He smiled with confidence as he held the black tag-it device in his right hand. "Of course, if you don't want to be tagged, you also have that choice. However, if you decide against it, you will be thrown into The Cell for three months. Once you arrive at The Cell, you'll be tagged anyway. But the choice right now is yours."

He had to make it seem like they did have a choice. He knew the truth: they had to do whatever they were told, not everyone would be able to handle life inside The Cell. Most borders learned to adapt but not all of them were able to do so.

The Cell had its uses. First, it was an adequate way to punish those who made an active decision to disobey the rules. Secondly, it would help The Agency strategically remove the weak. It didn't matter to The Captain if a border didn't make it out of The Cell alive. That would only mean that that person wasn't fit to be among the strong, devoted society The Agency was wholeheartedly determined to create. Sacrifices had to be made.

The woman's name was Scotia. She smiled up at him. "Do you need me to tag *you*, Captain?"

How bold of her to speak to him like that. The last thing he needed—or wanted—was someone creating a scene. He had to handle this delicately but what he really wanted to do was slap her across the face. Now was not the time. Maybe they'd meet again on terms that were more private and he could deal with it in his own manner then, when he would make sure no one was around to see or hear anything. It would be her word against a member of The Agency. Whatever he said would be deemed the truth. The girl would end up in The Cell if she dared speak of what had taken place. Trust among the people had to be earned. This was a good example of when to use caution.

He'd now taken notice of Scotia and soon she would be sorry. She was nothing but trouble and would need watching.

"It isn't necessary for members of The Agency to be tagged. But thanks for your support and the offer to help."

With that, he dismissed Scotia and grabbed Ted's wrist to place the chip in Ted's left pinky finger.

❖ ❖ ❖

As Ted was tagged, his eyes met Scotia's. He barely felt the pin prick as the chip was injected into his finger. She needed to back off, now. The last thing they needed was a member of The Agency following them around, thinking they were up to something. He was sure Scotia got his message that it was time to keep quiet. She turned away.

"What were you thinking, talking back to him like that? Do you want to spend time in The Cell? Not everyone survives there. I wouldn't be able to handle all of this without you."

Ted grabbed her by the shoulders. The last thing he wanted to do was upset her but this wasn't some game. Their lives were at stake. Everyone had to tread carefully. "Please be careful, Scotia. That's all I'm asking. Nothing less and nothing more."

"Sorry."

Ted knew this was all Scotia could force herself to say. Even though no one else was talking, there was no way everyone was okay with what The Agency was doing. Ted knew what she was feeling. While she was waiting in line to be tagged, he'd noticed Scotia looking around. The fear in everyone's eyes was real. Someone had to say something but he hoped it wouldn't be her. It wasn't much, but she'd acknowledged she was aware that what The Agency was doing was wrong. He hoped there wouldn't be repercussions.

As Ted and Scotia started back to their block unit, the crowd was growing louder and louder. Neither of them could make out what the fuss was.

"Leave it alone," said Ted. "It's none of our business. We've already been tagged. We're free to go and we should get back to the block. Whatever else is going on has nothing to do with us."

"We'll go in a minute. I want to know what's going on. Two minutes won't make a difference. And I haven't seen Brie in a while." Scotia's eyes locked with Ted's.

He allowed his sigh to escape. There was no use arguing. If he kept on walking without her, she'd stay behind to spite him. If anything bad happened to her, he wasn't sure how he'd be able to live with himself. She could be stubborn. One of the many traits she possessed that he admired. He didn't have any choice. He stayed.

3

"Captain, this one refused to be tagged." Member Brent exclaimed. He dragged the girl closer to The Captain with the help of Member Joe. The Captain would decide what to do. Brent was glad of that. He did what he was told. He didn't need any blood or guilt on his mind. At the end of the day, when he lay his head down, he would have no issues falling asleep. It was best for everyone if it stayed that way.

Captain Neal was not about to get himself or the people even more worked up than they already were. Power and control were vital. Things like this were expected to happen. It was impossible for everything to go smoothly all the time. Now and again, bumps would appear in the road. That's all this girl was, a bump. It was his duty to smooth things out. She would learn because she would not be given any other choice.

Not everyone could see the genius that was The Agency. Nevertheless, with time, they would learn. No matter what.

Captain Neal's smile widened. The timing couldn't have been more perfect. He scanned the crowd and what he saw pleased him: absolute fear. He had them scared. They waited, wanting to see what would happen to this bold girl standing in front of him as the drones circled.

"Ladies and gentleman, listen up. Let this be a lesson to all of you. It's simple. Follow the rules and everything will be fine. If you don't, there will be consequences. For example, this girl refuses to be tagged. As I said earlier, we all have choices. She's made hers." He paused for effect. It worked. Everyone fell silent. All eyes were locked on him.

Scotia elbowed her way through the crowd so she could get closer. She had to see what was going on. She couldn't find her sister, Brie. The Captain had mentioned a girl. She prayed that the girl he was talking about wasn't Brie.

✻ ✻ ✻

Ted watched from a distance. There wasn't much else he could do. If he followed, it would create a bigger scene. Keeping a low profile had worked for him so far.

"Member Brent and Member Joe, please take our new border to The Cell. She will remain there for ninety days. No matter what it takes, I promise you, she will be tagged. All this fuss is for nothing because in the end, you still lose." The Captain was no longer smiling. It looked to Ted like he'd had enough, that everyone was trying his patience today and it wasn't even noon.

✻✻✻

The crosses were silent. The Captain was acting creepy. It had been weeks since a new border had been picked up and taken to The Cell. This was definitely a spectacle worth waiting around to see. There was never a lot of entertainment in the City of Kneel. This was a good substitute and admission was free. Crosses knew from previous experience to part and make a clear path for Agency members to drag the girl by force to The Cell. Maybe she would be seen again but then again… maybe not.

4

The Member's grip was tight. It was becoming hard for Brie to breathe. Panic was setting in. This couldn't really be happening, could it? She wasn't sure what she'd expected but this was certainly not it. This wasn't good. Scotia would be devastated. She'd always said that one day Brie's smart mouth would get her into a new world of trouble. That summed up where she was currently.

Scotia, damn it. She had no idea how she was going to get word of her demise to her sister. Brie lifted her head. Perhaps she could yell and another cross could get word to Scotia. But just as Brie was about to yell, Scotia came into her line of view.

It was hard to accept, but this was even worse. She didn't want her sister to see her in her current state. And if something happened, and she didn't make it out of The Cell alive, the memory of this moment would forever haunt Scotia. The image would be permanently etched.

"Scoooooottttiiiiaaaa!"

It couldn't be. Scotia stopped a few yards away from Members Brent and Joe—and her sister. This was not a mistake. The newest border was her sister, Brie. This had to be a nightmare. Her feet refused to move;

they were paralyzed with fear.

She was beside herself. Nothing could be done. If she caused a scene, they would both be thrown into The Cell. She wanted to be with her sister and protect her as much as possible, but it wouldn't do either of them any good if she didn't have the support from Ted—and Tega— to make it through The Cell sentence. As much as it hurt Scotia, Brie was on her own. At least for now. Scotia could do more for her by remaining outside The Cell than inside it with her. She would think of something. She would have to.

❈ ❈ ❈

The Agents dragged Brie along. Her fight was mostly gone. Agent Brent was grateful for that, it was almost a two-mile walk to The Cell. The less she fought, the easier it would be on everyone. She was a strong little bugger. Lesson learned: you can't judge a cross by their cover. This was Brent's first border catch. He needed to ensure it went smoothly. If he messed it up, who knew what The Captain would do to make an example of him for the other Agents. Agent Joe had been around for a long time so this was nothing new to him. The last thing Brent needed was to use violence, but he would do what needed to be done—no matter the cost to the border. Agents trumped crosses in the City of Kneel.

They continued onward to The Cell. Brent needed to stay focused long enough to complete this task and then he could enjoy some relaxation time. This was good because he felt like things were starting to heat up.

❈ ❈ ❈

Ted tried to get Scotia to stand but she refused to move. She lay curled on the grass. He could hear her crying. It hurt him to see her like this but there wasn't anything he could do. The Agency had been around long enough for everyone to know that Agents ruled. It was the way things had been since he could remember, although the new Agency seemed to be taking things further. And not in a positive way.

If he couldn't convince Scotia to get up and move, the next best thing would be to sit and wait until she was ready. He couldn't drag her back to the block, and there was no way he could carry her. Even if he could, he figured within five minutes, one of the Agents would spot him. He would be stopped and there would be questions. The situation wouldn't look right to them. Anything out of the ordinary was suspicious and could land you in The Cell. The idea had been in his mind for less than three seconds before he dismissed it. He'd end up hurting himself or both of them.

Ted put his right hand on Scotia's back. To his disappointment, she turned, curled up even tighter and refused to even look at him. However, she did move in closer, which pleasantly surprised him.

She meant the world to him. Unfortunately, there was a good chance she'd never allow him to have more than what they had between them: friendship. It was best he didn't look too far into the future. *One step at a time.* Maybe one day Scotia would realize what she meant to him. Or maybe not. He had to accept whatever scenario he was faced with. There was no point in wasting what little energy he had. He should conserve his energy to deal with everything. The present moment was important so he should absorb and store it away for later. When he was alone, he could revisit the snuggle scene with Scotia. Lately, this seemed to be his favorite pastime: anything to do with Scotia Charles.

5

The Cell was located along the outskirts of the City of Kneel but within its walls. Close enough to be convenient, yet far enough not to be an eyesore—or have too many prying eyes. The Captain didn't want witnesses to the ugly things that happened behind closed doors. The Cell originally had been an old school but had not been used as such for over half a century. No matter what the weather was like, The Cell was always damp and cold.

Directly adjacent to it was an enclosed yard of about forty-five hundred square feet with barbed wire and chain-link fence to discourage borders from trying to make a run for it. So far, there hadn't been any confirmed reports of runaways. If there had been runaways, no one had lived to tell about their supposedly heroic escape. That was the point. The only way out was if The Agency granted that freedom.

The Cell was the place to send crosses when they had been bold enough to break one of the many rules. Visits from crosses from the outside were limited, usually one twenty-minute visit once a week. That was if the guards or The Captain hadn't taken take that privilege away along with everything else.

The Cell was a building smaller than one would have expected for its use. It was rumored to have a basement that was divided into two rooms. One room was used for food storage; the other was nearly empty, consisting of threadbare dusty blankets scattered about and a few metal pails. When a border fell out of favor with the guards, he or she ended up in this latter room, The Basement. If a border got sick, they were also kept in this same room, but under quarantine. It was a breeding ground for all manner of germs and ailments. Rumor had it that a border who had once protested the lack of food—or maybe it was when they had asked for a second helping at supper (who knew for sure)—had been sent to The Basement and was never seen again.

The Cell's main floor was large with a big kitchen, an interview room, a dressing room and a lounge room for the guards. The second floor was listed as a women's floor. It contained five cells with four women inside each one. The third floor was a men's floor with six cells and four men per cell. The fourth floor was another women's floor, an exact duplicate of the second floor. The fifth was a duplicate of the men's third.

Another little-used area in the prison was the attic, which was divided into two rooms: one empty and the other used by the prison nurse, Bev. There was also a large red shed outside. What the purpose of the shed was, no one seemed to really know.

The food was barely edible. The Cell was punishment, not a vacation. Crosses sent to The Cell were called borders. They were fed three times a day: oatmeal and a single cup of black coffee for breakfast; pasta with plain sauce and a cup of watered-down apple juice for lunch; and supper was generally two pieces of bread (not even toasted, which would have at least provided some variety once in a while) with a smidge of margarine smeared on it and a cup of tea at room temperature. Fridays were special because with supper they received a piece of fruit, usually a banana or an apple.

Whispers fluttered throughout The Cell. The borders knew something terrible was about to happen, something horrible and mandatory: The Calling. There was no set schedule for a Calling. Months could go by, and it was once rumored that two Callings had taken place within a week of each other. Borders had no idea when to expect one or even if they should prepare for one. People had survived The Cell but The Calling was a different thing entirely.

When they reached The Cell, Brent took in a couple of deep breaths. Joe said, "Ah. I get it. This is your first catch."

"Is it that obvious? I was trying to downplay that. All right, let's get this over with."

Brent took another deep breath, fixed his black suit and nodded at Joe. He was ready to go in. A good first impression was important. It would be imprinted. He needed to make it count.

With one hand holding tightly to the border—he couldn't let her get away, his career would be over before it even started—and his right thumb on the scanner clock, Brent quickly counted to five.

The clock turned green.

He was good to go in. The scanner clock kept track of who was authorized to go in or out of The Cell, kept track of time stamps and other information.

Brent and Joe entered The Cell with Brie.

Immediately, four cell guards in uniform turned to look their way.

One of the guards, named Blake according to his badge, asked Brent, "Is this new border for us?"

"It is. And a heads-up for her. Be careful. She's a strong one. The Captain himself decided she was coming here." Brent smiled. "This one thinks she's too good to be tagged with the rest of the lot. Looks like she'll be keeping you lads company for the next three months."

He handed Brie over as Joe held out the cert that was issued with each new border.

Brent's job was over. He had completed his mission successfully. Captain Neal wouldn't be able to find fault with him whatsoever. This was good. Perhaps he would be considered for a promotion earlier than he'd expected. This gave a much-needed boost to his confidence.

❃ ❃ ❃

Blake looked her up and down. This border was different. He could feel it. The cert didn't reveal much though:

Border's Name: Brie Charles

Border's Age: 25 years

Length: Aug 1, 2065 - Nov 1, 2065

By Order of: Captain Neal

Authorized by: Captain Neal

Most borders were somewhat unkempt, but not this one. This Brie woman seemed in fine shape. *In very fine shape,* Blake thought. She couldn't have been more than five foot five, barely weighed a hundred pounds, if that. He liked her long, dirty-blond hair and chocolate-brown eyes. At The Cell, he could pull rank. Usually, he didn't feel the need to, but for this one, an exception would be made. The name Brie somehow suited her, too. The long hair fascinated him. It was pulled back making the exact length a secret. But those eyes. He was curious what thoughts lay behind them. *This one's mine. And now I have a sudden craving for chocolate.*

❃ ❃ ❃

Brie felt the guards giving her the once over. A twice over in the case of one of them. It was not a good feeling being on display, being a source of entertainment. Their eyes lingered on her to her disgust, but she was at their mercy and would be for many days yet.

Stupidity. Nothing more than stupidity. Her sister, Scotia, had always told her that her attitude would get the best of her. She'd defied the Agents and now this was to be her home for the next few months, in well over her head. Best keep a low profile. No need to anger the guards or give them *any* reason to toss her into The Basement. Rumors echoed in her ears. She had no intention of finding out if they were true.

At least her sister knew where she was. Small comfort. Scotia was probably going out of her mind trying to figure out how to undo the damage. No matter the outcome, it had nothing to do with Scotia. This boiled down to nothing but ignorance on Brie's part.

"Brie. Your name is Brie," smiled Blake. "Well. Welcome. We're always glad to have new borders. It helps to keep things entertaining around there. Sometimes our routine get pretty monotonous. New borders always help in that kind of situation." His eyebrows went up. "You sure are pretty. But looks are not going to get you what you want in here. I'm the boss. Whatever I say goes. Whatever I want, you do, and you will do it, or else. Best to keep new borders on their tip-toes right from the get go." The smile was gone. "Answer me with Yes, sir."

"Yes, sir," Brie said, but only loudly enough for him to hear. She didn't like the way he'd used the word *entertaining*.

Kep had also taken notice of the new border. He was sure all the guards had. There was no way of missing her beauty. This one was definitely different. It was obvious it was her first time in The Cell. It would be memorable for sure. Guard Blake was always preaching to him that he needed to take more initiative with his work. Perhaps this was his opportunity… with Brie. It was better to step in before one of the other guards did or he'd be kicking himself later for another missed opportunity.

"Guard Blake, shall I take the border down to the dressing room?" Kep's eyes never left Brie's as he waited for a reply.

❧ ❧ ❧

Blake wasn't sure if he should take Brie down to the dressing room himself or let Kep do it. He wanted to get a better look at her, but at the same time, didn't want to appear too eager. And it was just yesterday he'd given Kep a big lecture on taking more of a lead instead of waiting to be told about everything that needed to be done. It was beyond annoying. No. More than that. Kep's laziness and the lack of ambition of the other guards, too, really pissed him off sometimes. There were always things to do at The Cell and Blake shouldn't have to be wasting his own precious time barking out orders to everyone else.

"Yes. That would be a good idea. Good for you taking the initiative like we talked about. Keep up the good work, Kep."

Perhaps it would be best if Blake took a step back for now. There was no rush. The girl would be here for a while. No rush. Slow and steady was the way—at least some of the time.

❧ ❧ ❧

Brie's entire body tensed. She wasn't sure if it was better or worse to realize that another guard had offered to take her down to wherever. Would they be taking turns?

7

When they arrived back at the block, Ted didn't want to leave Scotia by herself. She could be unpredictable, emotions wobbling back and forth. He just wanted to lie beside her and rest, for both of them to rest. Relationships took time. There was no need to rush into anything. A person couldn't help how they felt, Ted knew *he* couldn't where Scotia was concerned.

Scotia was beautiful and best of all, she didn't know she was. She was the complete opposite of her sister. She was nearly five foot ten, with auburn hair that danced just above her shoulders. Her eyes were something he'd never seen before and would mostly likely never see again: forest-green. She was nothing like any of the other women he'd ever met.

"Do you want me to stay?" Ted was hoping for a *yes*. "I know there isn't really anything I can do to help but I could keep you company. For a while? It's not much but..."

"It's my fault. I should've been watching more closely. If we'd arrived earlier, none of this would've happened."

"You mean if you hadn't waited for me, none of this would have happened." Not for one minute did Ted believe any of this was his fault.

If they'd been five minutes earlier or twenty minutes earlier, it wouldn't have mattered. Everyone knew it was only a matter of time before Brie's smart mouth would get the better of her. It was plain bad timing on Brie's part but the damage was done.

"That's not what I said. Don't you dare put words in my mouth, Ted. Don't you dare!" Scotia clenched her fist tightly and Ted saw her anger slowly rising. He knew she wanted to punch something. He knew she really did believe it was his fault. If he'd stopped reading right when she said they should go, none of this would've happened. But nope, he had to finish reading that chapter. He could never stop reading in the middle of a chapter.

"Scotia, in case you haven't noticed, Brie is her own person. Nothing you or anyone else says matters to her. Brie is impulsive and doesn't think things through before she acts. Whatever pops into her mind, she blurts out. I know The Cell is dangerous and this isn't a good situation. I'm not stupid. Give me some credit. And trust me when I say, blaming me—or yourself—isn't going to change a thing. This isn't going to magically disappear." Ted hoped he was sounding reasonable, but supportive at the same time. If anyone were to blame, first up would be The Agency. And second would be Brie herself.

"Do you have any idea when the last Calling was?" Tears streamed down Scotia's face.

Ted shook his head, no. He couldn't trust himself to answer with a solid voice. He'd forgotten that one horrid detail about The Cell. Brie was strong but if a Calling took place, her strength wouldn't matter.

"Me neither and that's what worries me." Scotia took a step closer to him. "I can't lose her. She's all I have."

"And me. You'll always have me. Please remember that."

"I'll check in with you tomorrow."

She walked away, hesitating in mid step which was enough for Ted to know she knew she was being unreasonable, knew that he didn't deserve to be treated this way, knew that it wasn't acceptable for her to be taking her anger out on him.

❋ ❋ ❋

Brie tried taking in everything at once. There wasn't a whole lot to take in, but she figured it was best to get to know the place. Kep, the guard, didn't look too tough. But that could be some sort of ruse to get borders to let down their guard. Maybe she could even overpower him. She didn't have a plan if she made it out though. Besides, Scotia had told her many different times that no one had ever escaped The Cell and lived to tell about it. If she were going to attempt an escape, a lot more thought and planning had to happen first and, obviously, now was not the time. She'd have to wait. She couldn't afford to be impulsive.

The first stop for a new border was always the dressing room which was at the very back of the main floor. This was where borders would be inspected.

They'd already walked down several barely lit hallways and she was scared. She'd never had what people call a panic attack but felt like she might have one now so tried controlling her breathing. Every time she breathed out, she would count to ten. She'd never been naked in front of anyone other than her sister and that didn't even count because they were related. Could she prepare herself mentally for what was coming up? Probably not.

❦ ❦ ❦

Kep tried to hide his excitement. He was anxious to get to the inspection room, after the dressing room. Normally, this part of the job could be a pain in the ass but not today. Today it would be rewarding.

He would try to behave professionally. "Step inside please." Most complaints from borders barely went anywhere but he couldn't take that chance. His record was clean and he planned to keep it that way.

❦ ❦ ❦

Brie looked at Kep. It appeared she was to enter the nine-by-nine-foot room first and he would follow. Strangely, there was no door to the room. Would she be naked in front of more than one guard? Not good. But if there wasn't a door, the worst that could happen was she'd be naked. Nothing else, so that was a relief. She was a virgin. The last thing she needed was some horny idiot to take that away from her. No one would want to be with her after that. There didn't seem to be a desire for used goods. Who knew if she would even survive this hell. But if she did, she'd need to maintain the hope of leading a somewhat normal life afterwards. It wasn't a good idea to look too far ahead, but at the same time, she needed a plan or she'd find herself going in circles.

Brie knew three things for sure: she had to remain hopeful, start planning for her future, and get out of this place as fast as possible.

nce inside the room, Brie waited for instructions. The policy inside The Cell was that borders were not to speak unless spoken to first. No comments. Answer the questions asked. No less. No more.

She couldn't take her eyes off Kep who currently had all the power and control over her. To say it pissed her off would be an understatement. She couldn't believe she'd been silly enough to let something like this happen. If only she'd listened to Scotia and kept her mouth shut.

❋ ❋ ❋

"I need you to take all your clothing off. Fold them and put them on that chair. After you've showered, I will inspect you. You'll put your clothes back on and then you'll be tagged. Take care of your clothes. That's what you'll be wearing during your stay."

Kep loved the look the borders always gave him when they found out they'd be wearing the same dirty clothes for the duration of their stay. In this case, ninety days. The first week usually went okay but after that, a disgusting smell would be a foul aura around them. By week three, they wouldn't be able to take it. They'd itch all over—an added punishment with no work required by the guards. A brilliant and inexpensive tactic courtesy of Captain Neal.

Kep's eyes never left Brie. He watched as she first took off her black lace up boots. Next the black socks came off. Feet naked. Next, the black jeans. He raised his eyebrows. There was a belt on her pants; it would have to be taken away. Borders were not allowed to have anything with which they could potentially harm themselves, guards, or others.

"Unfortunately, you won't be able to keep the belt, the boot laces, or your bra. It's against policy. When you put your clothes back on, leave those items behind. Nothing personal. It's a safety thing for everyone." Kep was having difficulty keeping his face expressionless.

Next he watched as she removed her shirt without hesitation. Nearly all female borders tried different tactics to stall with their top and even longer when the time came for them to remove their bra. But it honestly seemed like Brie was teasing him. Interesting, Kep thought to himself.

Brie stood completely naked before him. It appeared it hadn't been as unpleasant an experience for her as it usually was for most. Either that or she was good at covering up her feelings.

"Good. No issues. Another thing, the necklaces and earrings have to be removed. No personal items are allowed during your stay at The Cell. Another one of the rules but all your items will be returned when you are released." Damn she was good looking. Her breasts weren't big but not exactly small either. Just enough for a lucky man to grab a handful of.

Kep turned away to fill out the log form. It gave him a moment to rein in his thoughts. He could feel himself getting hard. Not very professional at all. He took a couple of deep breaths, bit his lower lip, and took longer than necessary to fill out the paperwork.

❅ ❅ ❅

Brie took off the sterling-silver moon necklace. They'd better give it back when she left. The necklace was special. Scotia had given it to her for her twenty-first birthday. Next, she took off her small silver hoop earrings. It felt strange to be without them. She hadn't taken them off in years.

Kep distracted himself by keeping busy double-checking the documents as he logged everything. He made Brie take a quick shower. The shower stall was completely transparent so guards could watch the borders' every move to make sure no funny business was going on.

He attached a little sandwich bag of personal items to the log form, placed it in an orange folder then stored it with the other borders' files in the cabinet which he locked.

"You can put your clothes back on. This part is done for now. After you get dressed, I will personally tag you. Is there going to be a problem with that?" He waved the tag-it device.

❃ ❃ ❃

"No, sir." Brie knew now was not the time to be defiant. She was alone, vulnerable, at the complete mercy of the guards. It hadn't even been two hours and she already felt like she'd been in The Cell long enough.

Scotia had always preached that things could be worse, and worse had arrived. She was now tagged. It hadn't hurt. A quick pin prick into her left baby finger and the deed had been done. If she hadn't felt owned before, she certainly did now.

❃ ❃ ❃

After the dressing room, it might be a while before Kep would be completely alone with Brie again. He would have to wait and control his patience. He wasn't in the mood to escort her to the quarters yet. Brie had intrigued him in more than a physical sense. There was something different about her. He wanted to touch her so badly. He couldn't ever remember feeling like this about anyone, let alone a border. Even a kiss would've been enough to hold him over.

❋ ❋ ❋

Brie knew now was not the time to be defiant. This had to be a joke, she was sure of it. She knew her time at The Cell would not be a vacation.

She looked at the room, it was maybe thirty-five feet square. Not bad for size—if there was only one person in it. But there were others. She'd be sharing it with three women. Four women had to share the same space.

The room was dingy. A single light bulb hung in the middle of the room and a piece of dirty gray string to turn the light on and off with came down from it. Four walls and zero windows, not good. Brie was already starting to feel claustrophobic. The string seemed hard to reach but then again long pieces of string posed a threat to the borders. It wouldn't look favorable for The Cell if borders attempted or succeeded in taking their own life or someone else's. Brie soon found out that during the night, guards would look in on them with a flashlight. Lights were off by 9:00 PM. After that, only darkness and silence carried them into a new day.

Right now, the others were sitting on the floor at the back of the room watching her closely. It was creepy but she guessed it gave them some needed entertainment. The first twenty-four hours would be interesting for sure.

One of the others was young. Brie had no idea of her age but not older than eighteen at most. What Brie did know was that the girl was too young to be in a place like this.

The girl pointed at what appeared to be a black sleeping bag. All the sleeping bags were black. Each border had her own. That was a bit of a relief. At least all four of them wouldn't have to share a scrap of cloth and play tug-of-war all through the night.

The young girl stood up and walked over to Brie. "Lights go off in a few minutes. Better be ready by then 'cause you won't be able to see. Not good. Stumble and make a noise? Guard's gonna come in and be none too happy about it neither."

Brie was surprised she hadn't realize it was so late. The other two women seemed older, more mature, but it was the young one who took charge.

Brie nodded. There didn't seem to be too much else she needed to learn about the room right now—except where the bathroom was. Maybe they had slotted times and the guards came to take them out or something.

"Thanks for your help. I'll get settled in a second but in case I need to use it later, where do we go to the bathroom?"

"In the bucket." Young Girl pointed to a corner in the room away from the sleeping area then lay down in her own sleeping bag, turning her back toward Brie.

Brie stared at what appeared to be a metal bucket. A large roll of paper towel was beside it. This had to be a joke. They couldn't actually be expected to squat over a bucket to pee or take a crap. It was a sign. Obviously she was sleep deprived. Things would look better once she got a couple of hours of sleep. The best thing would be to take off her pants so they didn't bunch up and wake her during the night.

"Best sleep with as many clothes possible." Young Girl jerked her head toward the doorway to their room. It didn't have a door. "It'll get colder. Safer that way, too."

Brie's eyes followed hers. She wasn't sure what the girl meant by safer but thought it best to take all the advice she could. Completely out of her element, she snuggled into her sleeping bag, hoping for sleep.

Time crept by. Although it didn't matter, it wasn't like she had some place to be. Just as Brie had finally started falling asleep, she heard one of the women sobbing. It sounded like she'd tried muffling the sound by covering her mouth with the covers, but it hadn't worked.

10

Brie felt a gentle nudge. Slowly she opened her eyes and blinked twice. She had no idea where she was. Nothing seemed familiar. She had a bad feeling in her stomach.

"They're coming soon with breakfast," Young Girl told her with exaggerated politeness. "Best if you're up and at 'em with your bed made or you catch trouble."

It started coming back. The day before. The refusal to be tagged. Scotia watching as she was dragged off to The Cell. Sentenced for ninety days for not doing as she was told. She wasn't going to let that happen again. She rose quickly and fixed her bed, somehow managing to make hers look like the others. Soon enough she'd get the hang of things.

She turned to Young Girl. "What's your name?"

"Sally. This here's Nancy and Mary."

The others nodded. It seemed Sally was genuinely the leader of the group.

A guard appeared. His name tag said Spry. Since there was no door, he just stood at the entrance to their quarters, holding a tray. "Step forward."

Sally quickly took the breakfast tray.

Spry turned and left.

Nancy and Mary moved in around Sally and sat down. Brie followed suit.

Sally explained the breakfast routine. "It ain't much, but this is what they serve every morning. Breakfast is always 'tween 6:30 and 7:00 AM. One of us always needs to be standin'. Waitin' for the tray. We try to take turns. If we ain't in place, the guard might not leave it."

Brie soon learned that one of best ways to keep on the guards' good side was to know what was going on at all times. Things in The Cell got hectic and there wasn't always time to explain. If you were a good guard, you were already in the loop and this helped make things run a lot more efficiently.

Things usually turned out better for everyone that shared living quarters if everything was kept at a calm level. If borders were too stressed or upset, it could lead to fights and other horrible things—like a visit to The Basement. Sally said she hadn't been to The Basement and prayed every night she would never be sent there.

Sally passed everyone a cup of black coffee; at least today the coffee was warm. Some days, by the time the food tray was delivered, it was cold and tasted gross but they had to drink it anyway. If the guards saw leftovers, they assumed you were wasting food and they may decide not to give you whatever item you were accused of wasting for a couple of days to teach you the lesson of being more grateful. Another reason to drink the coffee was because the food was limited. "Beggars can't be choosers." No matter how bad the food and drinks were, they had to take it. They needed every ounce of nourishment they could get.

Nancy handed out the bowls of oatmeal. It didn't look like oatmeal at all. When Brie took hold of the spoon to scoop up a mouthful, it was one big glob. She had no idea how she was expected to eat this garbage.

Mary let out a small laugh. "It's better if you pour some coffee in and mix it around. It'll take a few days but you'll get used to it."

Brie poured coffee over the top of the oatmeal and mixed it in, wondering why these other women were here. She supposed each of them would have her own story and in no time would be asking about hers. This probably wasn't the time to jump right into sensitive and personal information. She should try to focus on figuring out what was expected of her and tomorrow try to get information. Maybe they wouldn't even talk to her.

Even if they didn't want to discuss personal stuff, she hoped they'd want to talk about something. Anything except the rules of The Cell, or else every day here would feel like an entire month. No. She had to figure out stuff to keep herself busy or she'd lose her mind.

11

It was morning break, a few minutes away from the chaos of The Cell, and Kep was in the lounge with the other guards, catching up on gossip and enjoying a steaming cup of coffee.

Kep loved coffee breaks. They had one in the morning shift, and then took turns taking lunch and next a coffee break in the afternoon. If you did the night shift, you still got the same format, just at different times.

He decided on small talk. "She's quite the looker that new one."

"Don't none of you horny twerps get any funny ideas about her." Blake declared.

Kep stared at him with disappointment. Apparently he wasn't the only one interested in Brie.

The last thing the guards needed was a fight starting up to get around the new border. If that happened, Kep knew that Blake would put a stop to it before things got out of hand. That was part of his job, putting fires out. Sometimes it was between other guards, sometimes it was between borders and sometimes it was between guards and borders. One just never knew.

"Hey now," Spry asked. "So what does she look like, this new border that has everyone so riled up?"

"Seriously, why are you asking? Are you trying to be funny or are you just that obtuse?" Kep raised his eyebrows.

Spry took another sip of his coffee very slowly. He wanted to buy himself a moment to figure out if the other guards were playing a prank on him or if he'd missed something.

"You *are* serious," said Kep. "My gosh. Pull your head out of your arse. Stop daydreaming and pay attention. You saw her when you did the breakfast drop this morning. She's on the first women's floor."

The newbie guard would be teased about this one for the next few days. For a second, Kep felt sorry for him but that passed quickly. Spry had started gaining a reputation for being a daydreamer. This wasn't a good habit for someone working inside The Cell. Maybe it was a good lesson if the other guards teased him for a few days. Spry needed to learn to focus on his job.

❅❅❅

Spry felt his face turning red. Yep, just what he'd feared. He'd missed something obvious. Now if he'd been paying attention when doing his rounds earlier, he could be bragging to the guards about what he saw. But because he'd been wondering what she looked like, he'd missed out and would be the brunt of jokes during coffee breaks for what would feel like an eternity to him. Boy, was he kicking himself now. He could hear the laughter as he turned down the hallway. Tomorrow was his day off. Good. Maybe by the time he came back to work, everyone would have forgotten about his mindless mistake. Not likely, but hope never caused any harm.

❅❅❅

Kep wanted to see her again. Merely thinking about her was making his body react. He should have made a move on her in the inspection room. No one would have found out. New borders never complained, they were too scared to. At the same time, however, he knew that if he'd tried anything, and it wasn't wanted, he'd have ruined the chance of anything ever developing between them. A quick lay wasn't going to be enough. Kep wanted something more.

The Cell was definitely not the place to be daydreaming. That was what Spry's problem was, too much dreaming. Spry was a young lad, only nineteen. Kep wondered what he was always dreaming about. Maybe he had a special girl or something.

Kep had to come up with a plan to see Brie again. He hoped that over the next day or two something would come to mind. Maybe an opportunity would come up where he could gently touch or kiss her or something else to let her know he was interested in her. If he didn't make a move fast, it was obvious one of the other guards would. Brie was scheduled to be here for a while, but who knew what the other guards had in mind—or when the next Calling would take place. The guards never received much notice about dates for future Callings. He was sure the last one had taken place a couple of weeks ago. This meant there would be another one soon. Maybe he wasn't up high enough in the ranks to be privy to information of this nature. Maybe he should start paying closer attention to what was going on around The Cell.

Captain Neal took another sip of coffee. Maybe he should add a drop of Baileys to help clear his mind. He tried to keep his ear to the ground through the other Members of The Agency, making sure they remained loyal. Over the last few months, rumors had been flying around and had eventually gotten back to The Agency.

Didn't people realize by now that every word that was said circled right back to him?

There was no way they could risk anyone trying to leave the city. Kneel was independent and he wanted it kept that way. Obviously, they would lose some people, but he could live with that. It was part of the plan: weed out the weak so only the strong survive. With strong people, the City of Kneel would flourish and become even more powerful. Not even he knew what the future held. And, there might be an opportunity for The Agency—the one he was in charge of—to rise up and perhaps take more power from the rest of the world around them.

By making it mandatory for all crosses to be tagged, they would be able to track everyone's movements, plus a few minor other things. That was all it was designed for, for the moment, at least. That's what they were telling everyone.

As Captain of the Agency, Neal was aware that the best way for changes to be made was gradually. Especially when attempting to take away someone's freedom. Slow and steady. Some of the crosses weren't that smart. There was even a good chance they wouldn't understand what was going on until it was too late. *I came up with a great plan, didn't I? Ignorance is bliss.* Captain Neal would take advantage of the ignorance of the crosses as much as he dared.

But the part about the cross who had spoken out against The Agency hadn't been on his agenda. That had just fallen into place. And as it was meant to be, he'd made an example of her. He hoped all crosses would remember that as well as members of The Agency would. He wanted everyone to know he was serious and wouldn't take crap from anyone. *Take no chances.* As a leader, Captain Neal knew there would be bumps on the road and that was okay. *I'm off to a good start. One step at a time.*

12

Scotia tried to sleep. She had to process—and tackle—what had happened. She had to be well-rested, have as much strength as possible. She was alone with no one turn to. Ted was amazing but Brie's fate was not as important to him as it was to her. Tega was great but was in the same mindset as Ted. No one had as much at stake in this ugly nightmare than Scotia did. Brie was her sister, her responsibility. All she needed was a foolproof plan. Was that even possible?

Scotia knew that Brie had to be terrified. Brie was tough but she was now out of her element. This was real. The Cell would be her home for the next three months. She wondered if they were feeding her. She wondered if Brie was angry at her for being locked up while Scotia was free. It was heartbreaking just thinking of her sister in that filthy place, being watched around the clock.

There had to be something that could be done. Maybe tomorrow, among everyone, they could figure something out. Scotia couldn't see how Brie could survive The Cell for three months. She'd never be the same. Being there had to change a person.

Maybe this was some sort of joke. The Agency couldn't really go through with it, could they? It had to be a prank. Even if it were true, there'd be no way to actually enforce this new rule. It seemed as the months went by there were more and more new rules announced. If The Agency kept this pace up, it would be no time before crosses had all their freedom stripped from them. Maybe that had been their intention all along. It would be easier to control everyone that way. The Agency was up to something. Would she be able to find out in time to do something about it?

Anything posted on the town wall was official and Scotia had just watched The Agency put up an announcement: all accessories such as necklaces, earrings, bracelets or anything similar was now banned for all crosses. If anyone were caught wearing any of the accessories listed, they would receive a warning; and if it happened again, it would mean an automatic strike and the wrongdoer would be sent to The Cell. Then right after that announcement, another followed: anyone caught outside their block after dark would also be sent to The Cell.

They were now restricting what they were allowed to wear and their movements.

Of course these new rules didn't apply to members of The Agency. They were exempt from everything. They had the first and last word, no matter what.

It was hard for Scotia to remember a time when things hadn't been like this, when things had been normal. It was becoming overwhelming. Phone calls could be made from your watch but crosses had long ago assumed The Agency could listen and record conversations to use against them. Since then, the majority of crosses didn't bother making phone calls. If they wanted to talk, they showed up in person. As each day went by, it seemed as though they were losing more rights. What bothered Scotia the most was that it seemed like a lot of the crosses were willing to go along with whatever was happening without asking any questions. It seemed they didn't have any intention of fighting back. This wasn't good. Eventually, they'd reach the point of no return. Scotia couldn't let this happen. She had to do something. It wasn't in her nature to sit back and accept things just because someone said so.

Her watch vibrated. It was Tega. Maybe she'd seen the announcement on the wall, too. It would be good to hear her voice. Scotia missed her even though their relationship a.k.a. friendship had yet to be clearly defined. She wasn't sure if what she was feeling was a phase or something more. She cared about Ted but whatever was going on with Tega was emotionally different.

"Scotia, what the heck's going on?"

"I have no idea. I thought maybe you'd have more information than I do. This has to be some sort of prank. I mean, really, The Agency can't do this to us. This is against The Code. They can't do this. We won't stand for it. We have to do something."

"Like what? If we strike back, we'll all end up at The Cell. We can't help your sister if we're inside with her. Think about it."

Scotia's stubbornness was as well-known as Brie's mouthiness was. This entire situation was going to be challenging for everyone. "I can't talk now. I gotta go."

"Don't do this, Sosh," pleaded Tega. "Don't shut me out. You always shut me out when you don't want to deal with things and you keep everything bottled up. This is not healthy. It'll make you sick if you keep doing this. Please."

Scotia ignored Tega's plea and hit the stop button on her watch. As usual, she was on her own and had no one else to rely on. Praying wasn't going to help but it would be nice if she had someone she could count on for once. It was hard always being the one stepping in to help others and being the glue that held everyone together. There wasn't any point in arguing about it with Tega or anyone else. Maybe Tega was right, but she could also be wrong. Everything was overwhelming. What The Agency was doing was wrong. Being forced to be tagged was wrong. Being thrown into The Cell for every little infraction was wrong. The Callings were wrong and whatever was going on in The Basement was wrong. Scotia wasn't entirely sure what The Callings were, but she knew something really bad went on when one happened: rumor was that not everyone involved with The Calling survived. Maybe the way she felt about Tega was wrong. That her sister was in prison was definitely wrong. The way Ted felt about her was wrong.

Her mind was racing all over the place. She knew how Ted felt about her and she tried her best to ignore it but sometimes she couldn't. Not with him staring at her all the time. As long as he didn't try to do something foolish, like kiss her, she should be okay. She had no idea what her reaction would be if he tried that.

Scotia didn't have time to figure out a million different feelings and scenarios. She wanted to be with Tega but maybe she wanted to be with Ted. She would stop thinking about Ted in any other way except as a friend because she was sort of *with* Tega. Well, nothing was set in stone but they had kissed once. She wasn't sure how she felt about that yet. All Scotia knew was that she was feeling pressure from everyone and everywhere. She was being pulled in too many different directions all at once. She wanted to be left alone but, of course, someone always needed her for something. Right now, that person who needed her was her own sister, Brie, and Scotia would do everything she could to help her. No matter what it might cost herself.

❀ ❀ ❀

Ted had no idea how to change things. He didn't like feeling helpless like that. Brie was gone and there was no way to know if they'd ever see her again. Of course he felt bad about it, but there wasn't a whole lot he could do, was there? Other than make sure Scotia didn't do something she might regret and end up in The Cell with Brie. And that actually sounded like something she would do on purpose to help Brie escape. Ted would do his best to keep that from happening. Scotia was his whole world, there was no way he could handle losing anyone else. For him, there would be no purpose in life if everyone he loved passed away. He couldn't let that happen. He didn't just *want* Scotia in his life, he *needed* her in it. Without her, he couldn't breathe.

Ted tried to figure out what he could do to support Scotia while limiting his involvement. The last thing he needed was to end up in The Cell. He knew he'd survive if he got thrown in, but he didn't want to leave Scotia. He'd chat with other crosses and find out when the last Calling had taken place. It was a place to start. If one or two Callings had taken place recently, that would improve the odds for Brie making it through her sentence alive. Merely attempting to find out any information on The Calling would be challenging. The topic was forbidden. Ted had heard that someone had died and wondered if that was a common thing: death during a Calling. He had no idea what took place during those events, only that some members of The Agency placed bets. He hoped those rumors had been made up for entertainment—or just to make crosses fear members of The Agency.

After spending the entire morning making small talk with different people he felt he could trust, Ted got the answer he was looking for. There had been a Calling a week earlier. This was good. It would be better if it had taken place just a few days ago instead of a week but it was definitely better than one having taken place a month or two earlier. Scotia wouldn't see this piece of hope the same way he did. Not that he would blame her.

There was a good chance that Brie was safe for at least another week. Maybe even two weeks, but who knew after that. She had to survive an entire three months and during that time, there would likely be one or two Callings, but most likely even more.

He knocked on Scotia's door.

"Hey."

He hadn't expected to be grabbed in a joyful hug, but she looked horrible and calmly detached. "Hey yourself, did you get any sleep?"

"How the heck could I sleep knowing she's inside and I'm never going to see her again? What a stupid, stupid question. Seriously. Sometimes you should think before you open your mouth, Ted." Scotia stood staring at him with both hands on her hips.

Usually, Ted would just ignore the hurtful comments she flung at him. It didn't happen often but when it did, it stung. It hurt. Not today though, he hadn't slept much either and he hadn't done anything wrong. She had every right to be upset but not with him. No. "I'm sorry you feel that way. I came to see how you were doing. I see your anger is still aimed in the wrong direction. I managed to find out the last Calling was a week ago. Have a good day."

❧ ❧ ❧

Scotia watched Ted walk away. She couldn't believe he was really going to throw out that comment and leave. Ted had never behaved that way before. What was his problem? He had to see what she was going through. Scotia waited. Surely he wouldn't walk away for real. Any moment now he would stop, turn, look back and realize what a mistake he'd made. He would come to his senses and come back. There would be a few moments of silence and everything would be as it was before.

Only Ted didn't stop. He kept on walking. The jerk never looked back in her direction. Fine. She could play the same game. No way would she cave first. He would come to her. He could play that game but she played it better.

✿ ✿ ✿

It was hard. Ted wanted to look back. He wanted to see if she was still standing there waiting. He wanted to make sure she was okay. He was tempted, yes. He wanted—yes, needed—to know if she did care. It didn't seem like too much to ask. What was the problem anyway? He'd always been good to her, always did whatever she wanted. Maybe it was time to back off. Maybe she'd been taking advantage of him. He'd never tire of helping her but he had to think of Ted, too.

It took every ounce of will power but he kept going. One foot in front of the other, next step, next step. Finally, he was around the bend and no longer in her line of sight. There, he stopped to catch his breath. It would be best if he stayed away for a day or two. Or three or four. It wouldn't be easy but he'd manage to do this.

13

Crying was something Scotia was not overly familiar with, but she couldn't help it. She'd barely slept because of her concerns for Brie. She wondered if her sister had had any sleep, if she was being bullied, if a Calling had taken place. Too many thoughts and zero focus weren't getting her anywhere.

And then Ted, the only person she could have talked about this with, had walked away. How dare he! She would show him. She was strong and independent. Not that she had a game plan or anything but whatever was going to happen, she would do it alone, without any help from him. That was a fact. Even if she were dying and he was the only person around to save her, she would not ask for his help. She would rather die. She'd figure everything out on her own. She was probably being irrational but she didn't care.

✽ ✽ ✽

After breakfast, one of the women walked over to one of the metal buckets. There were two. The one all the way in the corner was used to relieve yourself. No privacy. Everyone knew your business. The second was closer to the door and contained water. A fresh bucket arrived every morning right after breakfast. This bucket of water was to be used to clean the dishes after eating. Handwashing or anything of that sort was to be done in that same bucket. Borders took turns at dish duty, collecting all dishes from all borders and bringing them to the kitchen.

Brie tried to hold it in as long as she could but finally it couldn't be avoided any longer. She would have to relieve herself—in front of everyone. Pride had no place in The Cell. It didn't surprise her that The Cell would strip her, take everything she had, piece by piece. She hadn't thought the tears would creep up so quickly. She thought she was stronger than this.

She eyed the bucket.

"Can't hold it in forever and if you try, you might make yourself sick. Just sayin'. Can't be helped. Part of being human. Ain't no shame in that."

Brie appreciated that Sally knew she was having trouble adjusting. She guessed they'd all had trouble when they'd first arrived. The sooner she could let go of her pride, the easier it might be.

"I know. But I don't want to." As soon as the words left her mouth, Brie wanted to kick herself. She should have kept her mouth shut. She sounded like a whiny kid and she had to remain strong. It was the only way she could survive this. It hadn't even been twenty-four hours and she was starting to crack. How pathetic.

❀❀❀

"I'm not sure what you did that got ya sent here, but I will tell ya somethin'. That pride of yours is gonna get you into even more trouble. I have 'sperience. Trust me on this."

Sally would leave her speech at that. She needed to look after herself. There was no time to babysit a new border. She hoped the girl would take her advice. That's all she could do to help.

❀❀❀

After the third glance over at the bucket, Brie decided she couldn't hold it in any longer. She had to pee.

She unbuttoned her pants, pulled down the zipper and let them drop to her ankles. Slowly, trying to stall as long as she could, she pulled down her underwear and crouched over the bucket. It was so beyond humiliating, she wanted to cry and she was so nervous, nothing was coming out. *Focus. Focus.* The last thing she needed was to fall on the bucket, tip it over and end up buck naked on the filthy floor, and in everyone else's pee. She shivered at the thought. *Stay calm. Everyone has to do what you're doing. No point getting yourself worked up. It'll be fine. You can get through this. One moment at a time. Stay strong. Stay strong.*

Finally, she managed to pee and just as she was wondering how she was going to stay crouched over the bucket and grab the paper towel to wipe herself with, she heard someone clearing their throat,

"Here. One person stays close by in case you need help. Like to pass you the paper towel." Nancy smiled down at her. "It's uncomfortable at first, but you'll get used to it."

Brie let her breath out then took the paper towel from Nancy and dabbed. The paper was rough; she didn't want to rub and end up scratching her private parts. The last thing she needed was a rash or infection. She was sure medical care wasn't a priority in this place.

"Thanks."

Once she was standing straight and her underwear and pants were back in place, she felt better. The experience hadn't been fun but it would be manageable next time. Now defecating in the bucket would be a lot more difficult. No point worrying about that. When she had to go, she would go. One step at a time.

14

In theory, the idea was brilliant. The only way to get rid of weak crosses was to slowly lower the numbers through punishments that included time in The Cell, The Basement and, of course The Callings. With crosses dying, there was a need to increase the population of Kneel or soon there would be hardly anyone left.

"But how are we going to find a way to ensure crosses don't get pregnant on their own?" Brent asked.

To Captain Neal, that seemed like a good question. "I'm working on that right now." Despite himself, he smiled. "Give me a little more time." He still didn't have a plan, but it would come to him soon. There were times he didn't like doing the things he did, but most of the time he didn't mind because there was never a day the same as the one before and, the biggest perk, not all the rules applied to him.

The Captain knew that to put one of his plans into action he'd need men he could trust. They'd have to not only be trustworthy, they'd also have to fear him. He'd have to ensure they'd do whatever was asked without question or resistance and the best place to go looking for these men would be The Cell.

The last thing The Captain wanted was to raise any red flags. On day seven he usually went over to The Cell to check in, to see how things were going, for an hour or two. This was the only way first hand to know what was going on, and to make sure he stayed on top of everything.

He always visited on day seven so there'd be no excuse for things not to be in order. But he always went at different times to add at least a small element of surprise. Next visit, he'd start taking more of an interest in some of the guards. The ones he would focus on first would be those in favor of The Calling. Not everyone agreed with The Callings, but striking fear into everyone in Kneel was a bonus. The Agency was powerful but they still needed "certain ways" to keep things in check.

❄ ❄ ❄

Brie decided it was time to push for more information. "Do any of you know when the last Calling took—"

Nancy lunged forward to cover Brie's mouth, whispering, "Don't ever talk about The... that thing. If the guards hear you, it's an automatic trip down to The Basement. We don't know what goes on down there but not everyone who gets sent down, comes back. We need to be careful."

Brie took a deep breath. She would definitely have to be more careful about what kind of questions she asked, of whom, and when. She'd forgotten that everything they said was probably being monitored.

"Sorry. I didn't know."

"Been over a week." Now Sally was whispering to her .

"What are we supposed to do all day? Sit around until we're fed lunch? Do the same while we wait for supper? Then go to sleep?" There was no way she'd survive if this was the case. She'd always kept herself busy. Outside The Cell, there were always things to do. Not to mention that the busier she kept herself, the less often she got into trouble. Keeping herself out of trouble was going to be hard so she needed to start working on that task as soon as possible.

"Today is day four," said Nancy. "Mostly, it'll be a quiet day. However, after supper, we will be brought to the bathing room. We're allowed an hour to get ourselves cleaned up. This only happens once a week. After supper, a guard will come and take us down. Bathing days are always good days, so enjoy it." Nancy smiled.

"Once a week? Cripes. Good to know." Brie preferred to bathe more often than that, but once a week wasn't the end of the world. At least there was something to look forward to. It would feel good to have water touch her skin. This wasn't exactly a place where everything was spotless.

15

Chatter rippled through the entire prison. Something was going on. Brie watched as Sally looked around nervously. This wasn't good. The noise meant something bad was about to happen.

Moments later, guards walked by each cell and looked inside. When one guard walked into their room, all four women stood still and held their breath. Maybe one of them was in trouble.

"I think you girls should be okay," Spry said and immediately left their room.

Nancy collapsed to her knees. "Whatever's going on, they don't want anyone in our room. Maybe I'll live to see another day after all."

Brie had to know. "What's going on? Is it The Calling? Is this normal?"

"Shhh! Nothing about this place is normal. I'm not sure. Probably."

Brie thought it best to keep quiet, follow the lead of her roommates. They had more experience.

About a quarter of an hour later, the guards walked by with two female prisoners. They weren't dragging them, but the women seemed hesitant. Of course, everyone had heard of The Calling. Anyone entering The Cell found out there was genuine fear of it within the first

49

thirty minutes of their stay. That was, if they weren't already aware.

Brie asked, "Nancy? Do you know those girls?"

Nancy's eyes went downward before answering her. "I'm pretty sure one of them is Audra. I don't know the other woman."

"The Calling." Sally's whisper was barely audible.

❋ ❋ ❋

Valter had no idea how he'd done it, but he'd survived. He actually pinched himself. *Yep, I"m still alive.* After being in The Cell for two months, he'd found out what The Calling was all about first hand. It was sick, disgusting, but it helped to control the population and was… "a source of entertainment." It had nearly cost him his life, but somehow, through sheer will power, he had survived. It would take weeks to recover—perhaps longer—but it would all be worth it.

There would be no more fighting. No more being at the bottom of the list of people's opinions. No more scrounging around for his next meal. Valter would no longer stare at the walls inside the prison. That was all gone and now he'd be more than happy to leave it all behind. This was the beginning of something new.

No. He wouldn't have to worry about food anymore. Or finding a place to stay. Nor would he have to be in those colored blocks with the others. No more low-grade crap for him, he was finally moving up in the world. He was excited about all the perks that would trickle his way but right now, the only thing that occupied his mind was that special meal coming up. Once he healed, he would be allowed to order any meal he wanted and he would take full advantage of that.

It had been a long time since Valter had eaten pasta. Fresh pasta with real meatballs and garlic bread with cheese. He was in his late thirties and ready to start the next chapter of his life. His stomach growled at the thought of delicious food. Yes. Maybe that would be his first real meal. And he would eat it every day for the next week. After all, he was important now.

A knock on the door interrupted his thoughts.

"Come in."

It was Bev, the nurse. She was smiling. "How are you doing today?"

"Damn good. Still sore but I'm sure that's to be expected."

"Glad to hear it. I'm going to check you over. Please lie down."

Valter eased himself slowly down onto the bed so he was lying flat on his back save for the pillow under his head. He watched her intently. She was good looking, beautiful even. Her eyes were emerald green. Her jet-black hair was cropped to her jawline. He was lying down so wasn't sure about her height. Probably five foot six or seven at the most. He couldn't guess her age, maybe mid-thirties to early forties.

"Does it hurt when I do this?" she asked, looking at his face.

"It's not too bad. I'll survive."

"I'm sure a couple of ribs are broken. If you want, I can bring you something for the pain when I bring you supper later."

"That'd be great. Maybe it'll help me sleep better. Is there any chance I can get some solid food tonight instead of soup and Jello-O?"

"It might be too early for that but I'll see what I can do, no promises. I'll have to check and see what they say. It's not up to me, I can only recommend." Bev looked a little sad as she finished his check-up.

✾ ✾ ✾

A guard showed up. Was he speaking directly to Nancy?

"Lice inspection today. You know the drill. I'll check back in an hour. Remember to inspect everyone thoroughly. No mistakes. And have someone check your hair as well. If anyone does, in fact, have lice, I need to know even if only eggs are found. Are we clear?"

Nancy replied quickly. "Yes. Perfectly clear. Thanks."

Brie looked at her. *Lice inspection?*

"Once or twice a week we have lice inspection. I've been here the longest so I'm in charge of doing it. We have to go through each other's hair thoroughly and check for lice and if there are any, report it. If you have eggs, it's not so bad. But if you have live ones, that's not good. They give you one chance to get rid of them. If, on the next inspection, you still have live ones in your hair, they shave off all your hair. What's even worse is that since they've shaved it off, everyone knows you had bugs in your hair. It's embarrassing."

"Lice. I never even thought of that. Another thing to worry about."

"Add that to your list of important stuff to remember, Brie." She turned to the others. "Who wants to be inspected first?"

"Since I'm new here," said Brie. "I'll go first. Mostly to get it over with. What do I have to do?"

"Take a seat and I'll go through your hair. It'll take a while."

16

Smiling, Audra made eye contact with an also-smiling Claudia as guards walked them out of the room. It felt good to be out in the fresh air. Then reality set in. Something had to be wrong. If a prisoner left The Cell, it was usually because their sentence was completed, but they still had time left to serve. Both of them did.

"All right, ladies," said Spry. "You have to keep moving."

Brent's insincere grin was wide. "The Calling. Aren't you gals lucky to have a second chance at life?"

"But what exactly is The Calling?" asked Audra. "What's going to happen?" She couldn't believe that Claudia hadn't said a word. There was no way she was going to sit back and go along with whatever was about to happen, either.

"Now you know we can't answer any of your questions," said Spry, apparently finding something funny about it all. "That's one of the rules. And it's probably better that way anyway."

Claudia and Audra kept walking along with the guards. What choice did they have? The guards were armed with small handguns and batons.

Spry remained vigilant. None of the borders had ever tried to escape on the way to The Calling and he wanted to keep it that way. These ladies seemed to know they didn't have a chance and weren't going along merely to learn what fate had in store for them.

❉❉❉

The barn was huge, red, dilapidated. Audra had no idea what it was for. She'd never heard anything about the barn from anyone, and that was odd because it must be important.

Brent reached into his pocket and took out his set of keys. One of them was large and red.

"Yeah," said Brent. "This building still uses a key system but it's on the list to be updated to the thumb print method they use for The Cell."

Audra looked over at Claudia who seemed to be as scared as she was. She'd never seen a guard use a key before; it was always a scanned thumb-print.

Claudia whispered to her. "I'll try to remember everything so I can report back to the other guys."

"I'm not so sure we'll have a zero chance of ever seeing the other guys again."

Brent unlocked the heavy door and they all went inside.

Audra smiled. Maybe she'd been wrong. In the middle of the building's interior was a table big enough to seat six people and set up with a red and white checkered tablecloth and two chairs. On the table was a small vase with what looked like a single red rose. She tentatively took a step forward but then glanced at Spry. Things looked promising but it could be some sort of trap.

"Go ahead," urged Brent. "Supper will be here shortly."

Audra walked over to the table to take a closer look at the flower. It was real. She could hardly believe it. Were things actually starting to look up? "Oh my. It's a real rose!" She clasped her hands.

Claudia moved in to stand beside her. Everything seemed okay, but Audra was certain that Claudia had never heard of anything like this happening before either. Audra was getting excited but she noticed that Claudia was taking a more careful approach.

The knock at the door made both her and Claudia jump.

Brent entered pushing a cart with trays of food on it. "Sit, ladies. Sit and you shall have your feast. You've earned it."

Claudia returned Audra's hug. They sat.

Brent brought the first tray over, and Spry brought over the second.

"Why don't you sit down and eat with us?" Claudia asked.

"No. It's okay," said Spry. "This is all for you. We hope you enjoy it." He continued to lay out the food: homemade shepherd's pie, gravy, spaghetti with meatballs, fried rice with egg rolls, blueberry pie, apple pie, pastries, milk and cola. The milk was cold and the glasses of cola had real ice cubes clinking against each other whenever they took a sip.

Audra's eyes wandered over the food, pondering what to eat first. Probably a croissant, but she didn't want to get too full before the main course and the pie. She hoped she might be allowed to save the pie for later. That way, she'd have something to look forward to. It seemed wrong to be devouring all this food at once. It had been a long time since she'd eaten anything like this. She wanted to dive right in but fear was building in her stomach.

"Gravy?" Claudia asked, holding up the porcelain gravy boat with a huge smile on her face.

"That'd be great."

Claudia poured gravy onto her plate then took sip of cola. It all seemed like a dream.

As they dug in, Audra attempted to divert her qualms about everything that was going on. The food was right here in front of her and there was no way she was going to pass it up. And something told her she should eat it; that she was going to have to keep up her strength for whatever might happen next.

17

It was day seven. Once a week, the borders were allowed out into the well-fenced yard as drones watched their every movement.

"Ten minutes," Nancy told Brie. "In ten minutes, the announcement will be made for us to go out into the yard. Remember. We'll only have twenty minutes out there."

Brie hadn't much hope, but she was still sure Scotia would come to visit. In a way, she didn't want to see her sister because it would be harder to walk back inside the prison and its reality. All told, Brie felt she was handling everything well. As well as could be expected.

"Is there anything I should know about visiting day? I don't want to mess it up. Especially my first one."

"There'll be guards patrolling the yard so careful what you say. Probably better if you don't mention anything that happens in here. No sudden movements like running because that'll look suspicious. It's not just the guards that'll be watching. Don't forget about the drones. Not sure how much they capture." Nancy shrugged.

Moments later they were in the yard. Immediately, the majority of the borders walked right over to the chain-link fence to see if anyone had shown up to visit them. It felt good to be outside. She'd only been

56

in for a few days and already she'd nearly forgotten how wonderful fresh air felt.

She walked slowly as she scanned the crowd outside the fence, looking for her sister. She was all nerves, scanning the crowd twice but didn't see Scotia. Her heart sank. She'd thought for sure Scotia would show. This was unlike her. Scotia had always supported her, no matter what kind of mess she'd gotten herself into. She had to stop entertaining the thought that her sister had abandoned her. She needed to stay focused.

Brie truly believed the only way her sister wouldn't show up to visit was if something had happened. She walked faster but there were so many people lined up along the fence, it was hard to pick anyone out. She still didn't see her sister but, surely, if Scotia couldn't make it, she would have sent Ted in her place. He would know what was going on. Brie started looking for his familiar face instead. There had to be someone here to see her. She felt like she was suffocating.

Just then Brie heard Scotia shout. "Brie. Over here!" Scotia was waving both hands.

"You came! Is Ted with you?"

Scotia looked down at the ground. "No. He was busy. But he sends his best."

Brie recognized Scotia's tell. Whenever Scotia said something and looked down, it meant something was off; she was lying. Scotia wasn't being transparent. They weren't off to a good start. They'd been talking for less than a second and her sister wasn't telling her the truth.

"Are you making out okay? How's the food?"

"I'm okay. Honestly. It's only been a few days. I hope things stay this way."

As Brie chatted with her sister, she realized that the noise level had lessened and she looked away from Scotia. Half a dozen guards were making the rounds. Three drones circled the yard. It was annoying.

"I'm trying to figure a way out of here for you," said Scotia. "But so far, I've come up with nothing."

"I don't think that's a good idea. Things are manageable at the moment. I think we should leave things alone. It's only for ninety days and it hasn't been that bad." Brie faked a smile to assure her sister but figured she probably wasn't buying the act. She *was* fine, just more terrified than she'd ever been in her entire life.

"But the last *thing* was a week ago," Scotia whispered. "That means there could be another one soon. We need to do something. They're not going to stop. They'll keep taking everything away from us, not happy until there's nothing left."

"The timing of those *things* doesn't mean anything. There's literally nothing we can do anyway. We need to leave it alone." Brie backed away from the fence, leaving the two sisters staring at each other.

The loud speaker came on. Visitation would end in two minutes.

Unable to hug Brie, Scotia put a finger through the small hole in the fence and motioned for her sister to do the same.

Brie smiled but as their fingers touched, it was too much. She couldn't let her sister, or anyone else, see her like this. She instantly pulled her finger out from the fence and turned away. She needed to stay strong. The minute she cracked, she'd be a sitting duck. She had to stay focused in a place like this. It was the difference between life and death. Brie couldn't take any chances.

"Until we meet again." Scotia smiled as her sister repeated the same familiar phrase.

✤ ✤ ✤

The last thing Brie wanted to do was go back inside the stuffy room but, of course, she didn't have a choice. If they could spend more time outside, it wouldn't be so bad.

After the visitation, Nancy seemed more quiet and withdrawn. Brie didn't want to upset her but wanted to make sure she was okay. Although Brie didn't know the other women that well, she believed all four of them should stick together.

"Did your visitor show up?" Brie asked. She'd been so busy trying to find her own sister and focusing on not doing anything wrong, she hadn't had time to pay attention to any of the other visitors.

Nancy placed her index finger on her lips and locked eyes with Brie.

Brie raised her eyebrows in a question then decided to leave the matter alone for the time being. Maybe Nancy wasn't in the mood to talk. She'd ask again later, after supper. If Nancy still wouldn't talk to her, she'd leave it alone. She wouldn't harass her. She had better things to do—like making sure she herself stayed alive and well until her sentence was completed. It was great if she had people to talk to, but her number one priority was herself, not making lifelong friends.

As soon as they got back to their room, Nancy glanced around furtively, several times, to make sure none of the guards were within earshot. Next, everyone huddled around Nancy.

18

Ted knocked.

Scotia opened the door and held it open, but didn't say a word. He gathered that she was trying to impress on him that she was not enthralled by his actions—or lack of actions. Ted could tell by the expression on her face, the scowl, that she was still upset with him. He had expected nothing less. However, he considered it progress that she had actually opened the door this time.

Tentatively, he asked, "How are you holding up?"

"I'm doing better now that I've seen her." She waved him in.

"What do you mean you've seen her? Who? Brie? Please don't tell me you went to The Cell alone."

"Yes. I went by myself. I don't need you to babysit me all the time. And as you can see, I made out just fine and I'm back in one piece."

"Scotia, you've made your point." He closed the door behind him. "Next time, please let me know when you're going and I'll go with you." He didn't understand why she had to be so stubborn. Then again, that was one of the many reasons he was attracted to her. If there was one thing Scotia wasn't, it was predictable.

A knock at the door made his eyes connect with Scotia's before she reached out to open it.

It was Tega who quickly wrapped Scotia in a giant hug.

This was the last thing Ted wanted, being around Scotia when Tega was present. So far, he'd done a good job of avoiding that situation. He knew they'd been good friends for quite some time, the best of friends. But over the last month, he'd noticed something different developing between them. Tega seemed flirty with Scotia. He didn't know what to do about that. The last thing he wanted was to make a fool of himself in front of Scotia.

✾ ✾ ✾

Scotia unlocked herself from Tega's embrace, her eyes briefly connecting with Ted's and she distanced herself from her friend. It felt strange to hug her in front of Ted. Things had been different between her and Tega since that one kiss. She wasn't sure how she should feel.

"And?" asked Tega. "How did it go with Brie?"

"Brie seems to be okay but it's only been a few days. Guards and other borders are around all the time, and since the guards are *always* within earshot, it's impossible to talk about anything private. I checked with some of the other visitors on my way home. Did some digging and found out there were recent Callings." Scotia's voice dropped to a whisper. "Somebody said two women were taken out of The Cell earlier today. Neither has finished her sentence, so they weren't being released."

"The more everybody knows about The Callings, the more we can be prepared maybe?" suggested Tega.

"I'm not sure yet how having this information would be helpful to anyone, but let's hope so."

✾ ✾ ✾

"She's right," said Ted. "We don't know yet if this information is good or bad"

The more Scotia talked, the more it calmed his nerves in a way. Maybe she'd notice how supportive he was. Whatever he could do to help Scotia, he would. If only she knew how much he cared. Maybe one day she'd give him a chance.

"Probably bad for the women they took today," said Scotia. "But probably a good sign for Brie. If they took two people out today, they might wait a week before they take more out. Or even longer. This means I have more time to come up with a viable plan to get my sister out."

"Not sure I agree," said Tega. "Don't you think the best plan would be to let her do her time? I'm not sure it'd be a good idea to interfere. It's only for ninety days. You said she seems to be doing okay. Brie's sentence will be over before you know it."

"No. I am not going to sit back and wait for something to happen— or not happen—to my sister. I can't take that chance. I need to come up with a plan. Of course you guys don't care because it's not *your* sister stuck in cell hell." Scotia opened the door. "I'll ask you both to leave now, please."

❧❧❧

As Scotia's door closed behind them with a loud *snick*, Ted and Tega, neither of them surprised, stared at each other in silence.

"We can't let her do anything impulsive," said Tega. "You know how she can be."

"I don't know what to suggest. Once Scotia has her mind made up about something, it's almost impossible to get her to change it."

"At least we're on the same page about that." Tega walked away.

19

The borders were almost finished eating. Good. Brent wanted this part to be over with as quickly as possible because he didn't feel comfortable about anything connected to The Calling.

He was determined not to let anyone or anything hold him back so always put on an act for the borders, and more importantly, for the other guards, pretending he was in favor of The Calling, but it was the opposite. He didn't understand the reason for it in the first place. It seemed like the borders were only being set up. They fed them, were nice to them, then basically tortured them. Regardless, he would do what he was told—or he could be next. Survival of the fittest was how things worked in the City of Kneel. You would either kneel or keel.

Brent noticed that Spry was waiting for him to make the signal: a swoop of the right index finger into the air meant it was time for the next part. Nothing else was to be done until Brent made the signal. Eventually, one day, Spry would be the one who made the signal and someone else would be following his orders but for now he was still learning.

"I'm so full, I can't eat another bite," said Claudia.

"I know. This is the best meal I've ever had." Audra wiped her mouth with a rose-printed paper napkin.

"Do you think we'll be eating like this all the time now?"

"No, I think they're just trying—"

Brent reached out to grab Claudia's left hand, pulling it hard enough to cause her to stand. He made the finger motion and Spry rushed over to repeat Brent's movements with Audra.

✿✿✿

At the opposite end of the building, just outside of it, was a smaller building, almost like a shed.

Without Claudia even realizing what was going on, she was handcuffed to a big metal loop that was secured into the wall. She watched in horror as Spry did the same thing to Audra.

Claudia had enough room to stand up or sit down but the metal chain didn't allow for much other movement. She didn't understand the purpose of being given a fabulous meal and then being chained up. But then she spotted the two cameras mounted in upper corners of the shed, facing her and Audra. Were the guards going to take turns raping them or something? *Oh my God. I can't believe I let my guard down.* This must have something to do with The Calling.

"Hey, I thought we were free now," she called out. "What are you doing? This doesn't make any sense. I demand that you tell me what's going on. Right now!" She shook her free fist.

Claudia and Audra were about six yards apart, both chained to a metal clasp with only a yard of movement because of the steel chain. It was clear that neither of them was going anywhere. Claudia had been right all along. All that delicious food had been too good to be true. They'd been paid with food and now someone wanted something in return. Nothing could have prepared her for what was about to happen.

✿✿✿

"Guess what?" Brent silently counted to ten to help ground himself before continuing. "Now is the time. Now you get to find out what The Calling is all about. As you can see, each of you has been led to the shed. There are monitors…" He pointed at them. "… so you can be watched from the command station. That's where members of The Agency can watch from and place their bets."

"Bets?" said Claudia. "What are you talking about? Bets."

"What are they betting on?" asked Audra, voice shaking. "What do bets have to do with us?"

✽ ✽ ✽

Brent collected himself. He was already being watched by The Agency and the guards. He needed to be seen as calm and willing to do whatever was needed to complete this. Even if it did make him sick to his stomach.

He continued. "They'll be betting on you. Some will bet on you, Claudia, and others will bet on you, Audra. As you can see, to the right of each of you is a bucket of different-sized stones. From here on out, there will be no more food and just one cup of water. It's only one cup, so be careful. You wouldn't want to spill it. You'll need every last drop. There are no bathroom breaks. Nothing. Only one person will be alive at the end."

"What are you talking about?" Audra yelled. "What are we supposed to do? Stay here? Chained to the wall? Starve to death?"

"The option of what to do is up to you. The rocks are to be used to hit your enemy. Eventually, one of you will succumb to your injuries. The more times you hit your enemy, the more damage will be done, thus the weaker they will become. The person who is still alive at the end will be declared the winner of The Calling." Brent hated this part. "I should warn you. If you try to work as a team, it won't happen. Without food—and that small amount of water—you'll only last so long and it'll be an unnecessarily painful death. It's better to use the rocks and get things over with quickly. From my observations, that's the best way. Of course, you each, yourself, must decide on your own what you want to do."

Brent took a moment to briefly lock eyes with each woman, wanting to provide them with a small sliver of hope. "There is one piece of good news. If you win The Calling, you'll have literally hit the jackpot because this will mean your sentence is considered complete and in return, you'll receive free food for the rest of your life. We'll also look after your recovery, and once you're healed, you'll be free to go."

Brent clasped his hands. "It's officially midnight so we can start. Good luck to each of you."

With that, he walked away.

20

Then it was Claudia who started yelling. "You can't do this. You can't just leave us here chained up like animals. Please don't do this. I'll do whatever you want. Just don't do this. Please, I'm begging you. You can do whatever you want." She tried to control herself but the sobs erupted anyway.

Several moments later, with some energy already spent, she lowered herself to the floor. No use. He was gone and obviously didn't care. None of them cared. This was all fun and games to them and this time wasn't going to be any different. It would always be them versus us.

Claudia glanced in Audra's direction and there was the bucket of rocks just as Brent had described. The bucket was filled with stones of different sizes. On the left was the water. All she wanted more than anything else in the world was to have a big gulp of water and cover up with a blanket and go to sleep for the night. That wasn't going to happen. She was probably never going to enjoy a good night's sleep ever again. She was so very tired but if she fell asleep, it could lead to her death. That was a chance she could not, would not, take.

"It can't be true." Audra's voice quavered. "What are they expecting us to do? We aren't really going to start pelting stones at each other.

We're friends."

Claudia took a deep breath. She didn't know how to respond to that. She needed time to think. Time? She wasn't sure how much of that she had. The last thing Claudia needed was to say something to make the entire situation worse. She wasn't sure how she could manage, but didn't want to upset Audra even more.

❄ ❄ ❄

When Captain Neal walked into the room, everyone stood immediately as was expected of them, and no one would sit until he gave the order.

"You may be seated. How long have the women been in there?" He always scheduled The Callings to begin at midnight when most of the prisoners would be asleep and the guards would be at their posts. He expected Brent's instant reply to his question.

"Midnight, Captain. We started right on time. They've only been in there for a few minutes. Nothing yet, except the usual."

Captain Neal couldn't help but chuckle. The people who participated in The Calling always embarrassed themselves as they yelled, cried out and even tried to bargain their way out of their situation. It didn't matter what they said or did, they'd be forced to participate no matter what, if they wanted a fighting chance.

Captain Neal saw Brent's face tighten. "We'll start placing bets on who you think the winner will be. Spry? You've been here over six months now, correct?"

"Yes, Sir, Captain Sir. It was six months two weeks ago."

"Good. Get over here and get in on the action. All you have to do is let Badger know how much you want to bet and on whom. I don't have any tips to offer but make sure you can afford to lose whatever you bet. This is a game, which means there's a chance you'll lose."

He laughed as Badger wrote "Captain Neal" at the top of the large whiteboard used to keep track of everyone's bets, the amounts and what amount the pot was currently at. They used a whiteboard because it was easier not to leave evidence because it literally got wiped away. The largest pot to date had been around ten thousand dollars, nearly a year's salary for some people. The Captain provided food vouchers for every employee so none of them ever had to worry about food or shelter. In addition to the vouchers, each employee received a weekly stipend of a hundred dollars. That was why it was easy to get employees: he provided a rich life style.

Captain Neal shook his head. "Not this time, Badger. I'm not placing any bets. Sometimes it's good just to sit the odd one out."

"Okay, Sir." Badger erased The Captain's name and continued writing the other names.

Neal checked the time. Fifteen minutes had gone by. "Another five minutes for betting and then we'll close them down and get ready for the action." He poured himself a fresh cup of coffee.

The large monitor was already on.

"Is the volume on Badger?"

"They screamed and yelled for the first minute, Sir, but they've been silent since."

To be expected, thought Neal. *Eventually, someone will throw the first stone. That's the way it always goes.* He took a sip of coffee, then said, "It's time for a new list, Badger. We've had some new borders admitted recently and I want to make sure we're on top of everything."

Captain Neal watched as Badger took notes. He never seemed to have much to say but that was one of the reasons he'd chosen him for some of the dirtier jobs. Badger never questioned him and that's what The Captain required. He didn't have time to explain every little detail to everyone. People needed to do whatever they were told.

Neal took another sip of coffee. He stared at the monitor. Nothing yet. Both women remained seated on the floor.

"I like our pattern of alternating genders, so I believe we'll keep that up. The next pair for The Calling will be two men, next two females and so on. There was a new arrival sometime in the last week or two. I can't remember her name, but I signed the cert. Her name reminds me of cheese." He sipped again, eyes still on the monitor. "I'll need the list of any female arrivals in the last two weeks. I want to find her. I think she might be a problem moving forward and I want that fixed ASAP."

Badger, who had been faithfully taking notes, stopped.

Neal smiled and set his coffee mug aside. "I think she should be one of the next contestants. We can't have people like her disturbing the peace, can we? The audacity of her to question me. I don't think so. I can't let that happen."

Badger added a few more lines before he shut down his link-pad that served both as a cellphone and minicomputer.

"Please have the information I asked for ready and on my desk within the next seventy-two hours."

"Yes, Sir."

21

Claudia couldn't hold it in any longer. She had to pee but didn't know where she was expected to do that. After hearing one of the guards mention that people were betting on them and watching, there was no way she was going to remove her pants to do it so she closed her eyes and, humiliated and helpless, let warm, wet urine trickle out of her.

Audra still sat quietly in her spot. It appeared as though she was inspecting her nails. Strange. What bothered Claudia the most was that Audra seemed so calm. It annoyed her. Did Audra know something Claudia didn't? With that thought, and with the added humiliation of having just peed her pants like a little baby, Claudia was angrier than she'd ever been in her entire life.

Before she realized what she was actually doing, she picked up a large stone from the bucket. She waited to see if Audra had witnessed this movement. It seemed she hadn't. In that case, now would be the best time to catch Audra off her game. The guard had said only one of them was getting out alive. It was going to be her, not Audra.

Claudia stretched her arm back then hurled the stone in Audra's direction.

"Ow!" screamed Audra as the rock connected with the side of her head. Instinct kicked in and Audra ducked down to protect herself. The rocks didn't stop.

* * *

Captain Neal smiled. Finally, The Calling had started. The first rock had been thrown. He hadn't placed any money on the game this time, which was too bad because it looked like he would have made a wise choice. He had guessed it was going to be Claudia who would strike first. She was more vocal and had more gumption. Audra seemed to be a timid mouse who followed along with everyone else. That was good in some ways, but not so good in a lot of others. Survival of the fittest was what mattered most.

The rest of the members cheered as the match continued. This was The Captain's cue to leave. He enjoyed being around for the start of The Calling but after a couple of hours, it was boring, and toward the end, it was ugly. The middle and the end were the parts he didn't want to see. He just wanted to know the outcome, who won. It was time for him to go sit in his cozy office, have a drink. He knew he would be kept updated.

* * *

The next day came and went and no one had come to notify Captain Neal as to who the winner had been. It wasn't until the third day after The Calling that he was notified. Agent Em was the one who brought word. The Captain made a call to Badger for more details on the outcome of The Calling and the events and subsequent result had surprised even him and he wasn't easily surprised.

"She surprised us all, Captain. It looks like she planned it out. She got hit hard several times and eventually it looked like she fell over." Badger paused. "We followed policy and waited. Believe it or not, just before the three-hour mark was up, she got up like she hadn't been touched. By then, the other girl was asleep so she used that opportunity and she just whipped those stones and rocks. Next thing we knew, the other girl's head connected with the bricks. That's when her head split wide open. She didn't blink about it. She kept going. Truth be told, Captain, it was one of the finest matches we've ever seen."

"So, it's true then. Audra won The Calling?"

"Yep. Who knew she had it in her?"

Neal was certain that once Audra was able to eat a proper meal, she'd order the usual: cheeseburger and fries, but it didn't matter to him what that meal would be. Bev would see to it that the girl was looked after and got what she both wanted and needed. Surviving The Calling didn't guarantee freedom after all. One of the secrets he generally shared only with Nurse Bev.

22

Bev was ready.

"Captain, would you like me to do the usual?" She knew her part by now but always thought it best to stick to the same script. There was no way things could continue like this forever. It was already too much for her on most days. Things were falling apart fast. She now feared for the human race.

"I haven't decided yet," said Captain Neal. "This one might be a good one. We all know we need more good ones. Sometimes I don't give you enough credit but I do appreciate everything you do to ensure things run smoothly."

She recognized the smile. She knew he needed to make sure his staff was happy, that he needed to keep the members of The Agency and the guards on his side by giving credit where credit was due. He had to.

"Got it," she replied. As if there were any real choice in the matter. She'd been around long enough to know what happened to those who crossed The Captain: they suddenly disappeared, or were forced to participate in The Calling. She couldn't take that chance. Maybe if she obeyed enough orders, she could somehow buy herself out of this situation; or with enough time, things would change. She wasn't sure what she could do after all the time she'd spent with The Captain, but she hoped there'd be something. Every night before she tried to sleep, she prayed that tomorrow would somehow be different.

After a Calling had taken place, it was Bev's job to clean up the mess, making sure everything was kept under wraps. The Captain mandated some of the guards to help with parts of the clean-up. That was something, at least. She despised how much power he had over everyone. It was hard to believe that once upon a time things had been drastically different. This was the only thing that gave her a shred of hope that perhaps things could be like that again.

When Bev arrived, she was happy to see that two guards, Marcel and Mane, were finishing up and, moments later, Badger showed up to give quick instructions on where they were to be going.

It was Marcel and Mane's first Calling clean-up. Bev wondered if she'd ever see them again. She knew what happened to the bodies; they had to make sure there weren't any traces left so any number of lies could be spun to family members. "They ran away." "They had some sort of contagious disease." "Their heart gave out."

Bev could recite the list in her sleep.

She watched as Badger led the men with the body out back toward the prison. Right behind the prison was what appeared to be a shed-like structure. Most people assumed it was a big outhouse, or something of that nature. Bev knew better though. The shed was where the boiler that helped heat parts of the prison was. This particular boiler sometimes consumed wood logs—and sometimes, like today, it burned all traces of a dead body. Evidence literally went up in flames. Claudia would be gone forever. Someone on the admin staff would destroy her file. It would be like she never existed.

✤✤✤

But Bev's job was not to look after the dead, it was to focus on the living. She bent over Audra. It was best to take a cautious approach. Generally speaking, the winner of The Calling was either really pissed off and might attack, or they were happy, believing their days of being stuck in a prison were over, that they'd won their freedom. Either way, the winner was never in good shape, mentally or physically.

Bev observed the woman named Audra who sat on the shed floor, legs pulled up, head bent down into one arm because the other one was chained to the wall; she was shivering. Bev was used to the smell that came with the participants of The Calling. The winner always smelled of dirt, urine and sometimes even feces.

While Bev cleaned up the mess after The Calling, the guards cele- brated. The guards who'd won bragged and talked non-stop about why they'd made the decision to go with their particular bet and what they planned on spending their money on. This annoying chatter would con- tinue for a few days then eventually die down—at least until the next Calling when the whole cycle would repeat itself. She wondered if the disgusting cycle would ever be broken.

She did most of this part herself because the guards hated the par- ticipants and usually treated them cruelly. It wasn't like it was the guards' fault or anything. The blame lay with The Captain. However, everyone played their own part, following orders out of fear and the need for survival. Exactly what Bev was doing.

Bev touched Audra's hand, the one still chained to the wall. The girl barely moved. Bev touched her gently once again.

"Audra? It's finished. Everything's going to be fine now."

Slowly Audra lifted her head and stared at her.

Bev knew Audra would need more than a moment to clear her head, to decide if this had been real, or if she were still locked in the nightmare. "It's over. We need to get you cleaned up."

"I'm alive. I made it. But that means Claudia…" Audra sobbed as the fate of the other woman became clear to her.

"Shh. Let's not worry about that right now. We need to concentrate on you." All this had to be handled quickly. The last thing Bev needed was for The Captain to show up to see if everything had been taken care of, if Bev had completed her part. She was still on The Captain's good side and for now she planned to keep it that way.

Audra perked up when Bev removed the handcuff and almost seemed to relax when Bev helped her onto a stretcher.

"Lie down and try to relax. You'll soon be moved to a nice clean room."

Audra lay back, closed her eyes and remained silent.

Marcel and Mane showed up. As they carried the stretcher away, Bev heard a soft "thank you" from Audra.

For what? she thought.

23

Bev walked behind the two men as they carried Audra on the stretcher. As per one of the many unwritten rules, they entered through the back door of the next building and immediately brought her into a large bathroom. This was always the first stop for the winner. They needed to get them cleaned up.

The room had a huge step-in tub that was strictly for the survivors of The Calling. Bev put the plug in then turned the water on. Next, she added a capful of strawberry/chocolate-scented liquid that turned into bubbles. She checked the water temperature. *Lukewarm. Perfect.*

"You ready for a nice warm bath?" Bev asked.

Audra glanced around the large bathroom. "Is this all for me?"

"Yes. It's all for you. You've earned it. It's time to get you cleaned up. Start a new chapter in your life?"

Audra nodded.

Bev helped her into the tub then down onto the bottom step where she sat carefully and closed her eyes. The water probably felt amazing.

Bev watched the tears sliding down the woman's cheeks. She couldn't stand to be around her now. She felt like crap leading the girls on like this, thinking everything was going to be fine from now on. The truth was, sometimes they didn't live to see another day. It all depended on The Captain's orders.

Bev took a couple of deep breaths. She needed to stay focused. It wasn't like she could refuse this job or any others handed to her by The Captain. It was just the way things were. She hoped that would change. And soon. As each week went by, she was finding it harder and harder to sleep. She knew it was guilt from the role she was forced to play.

"I'll leave you alone for a little while to wash up while I track down fresh towels and a change of clothes for you. You have soap, shampoo and a cloth. Is there anything else you think you might need?"

"A brush or a comb would be great." Audra replied with a smile.

❈ ❈ ❈

Audra was sore and it would take a while to recover but it was looking like she was going to have plenty of leisure time for that. Then suddenly, the guilt of what had happened began to creep in. She quickly pushed it aside. *Not now.* She needed to relax. She had the rest of her life ahead of her. She wanted to enjoy this one luxury as much as she could. She hoped she'd be able to stay in the tub until the water turned cold. She wanted to enjoy every last second of this bliss.

❈ ❈ ❈

After supper, all the women in the room gathered around to chat.

"Why are *you* here?" Brie asked Nancy while she kept her eyes facing toward the doorway in case any of the guards appeared.

Nancy smiled. "I kicked an agent in his junk."

"What?"

"I was at the market buying veggies when I noticed an agent was walking around. Like, staring at me. He came up to me and got really close. It was gross but I stayed where I was. The last thing I wanted to do was anger him. Next thing I knew, he was feeling me up. I tried to pull away. He didn't like that. He grabbed me. Without thinking, I kicked him. In his..."

Brie stared at her. Surely, this quiet woman who sat before her was making this story up.

The other two women nodded.

"The agent went down like a sack of potatoes. The look on his face was priceless. But here I am. They brought me in a couple weeks before you. I got ninety days."

"Totally unlike me," said Brie, "but I think you've rendered me speechless for once in my life." She laughed. "Too bad you weren't with me before I got *my* ninety days. We might have been able to keep each other out of here."

Nancy shrugged. "Let's not go around regretting. It's bad enough here. I can't believe how disgusting the members are. And the guards. They believe they have the right to do and get whatever they want. They don't care what happens to anyone else. They see something they want, they take it. I just got tired of it."

24

There weren't a lot of perks to Bev's job but at least they gave her a small bottle of Baileys every week with her stipend. The availability of alcohol in the City of Kneel was low. The gift wasn't a lot but it was something. The alcohol also helped at moments like this. She didn't know what to do anymore. She splashed some of the Bailey's into her coffee. The lid was almost back on the bottle before she changed her mind and decided to add a second splash, *Just for tonight,* she promised herself. The last thing she needed was to start relying on alcohol to shut her thoughts up. She stirred the coffee, unsure how much longer she'd be able to keep this up.

The worst part was that Bev knew what was going on and the second-worst part was she had no one to share her feelings with. The guilt and the shame were eating away at her. The Calling was just plain cruel. How much longer could the details of it be kept secret? She was surprised The Agency had gotten away with it for this long. Over a year. How could The Callings be stopped? Everyone was afraid to speak up, herself included. She went along with it because she genuinely feared for her own safety but this, what she did to "clean up" after a Calling, was also her field of work. This was the one thing she had left in her life:

looking after other people. She'd already lost everything else.

She was an only child. Her parents had died in a car accident years before The Agency had taken over. She'd been working at the hospital when someone from The Agency approached her with an offer to work with them. She had agreed for two reasons: the pay, and most important, she thought by taking the position, she'd be privy to information that would allow her to be in the loop, be aware of what was going on and this would give her an advantage.

She looked into her cup of coffee. Half of it was already gone. *Slow down, make it last.* But she got up and added more coffee anyway. She considered another splash of Bailey's then changed her mind. *It's always best to have your wits about you.* The only time Bev felt like she wasn't on guard was when she finally fell asleep at night.

This was not the job Bev had signed up for. She was a healer, a nurse. Her purpose was to help people, not deceive them. *And once in a while even lead them to their death?* She really believed she didn't have a choice and wondered what would happen if she refused to continue. Her mind wasn't in the right place to think about that right now. She couldn't afford to make a wrong decision. For now, she had to continue. Did she have the strength to continue? To maybe one day make a real difference?

Then there was Valter. For one reason, she was worried about what The Captain's plan would be for him and for another reason, she seemed to be falling for him. He was around her age. According to the link-chart, he was in his late thirties. His voice was calming and he was tall, good looking with his coal-black hair and piercing green eyes. Was it her imagination or was he always staring at her? She was sure he blushed every time their eyes connected, so perhaps he was. It was very unprofessional but she couldn't help herself. He was perfect in every way, except they were on opposite sides. Nothing would or could ever happen between them. She had to make sure of that. Somehow.

25

*A*udra woke up screaming. She couldn't believe the nightmare she had awakened from was only that: a nightmare. She swung her legs off the bed, sat up and looked around the room. Nothing was familiar. Where was she? She counted to ten, trying to settle her nerves.

As she calmed, little by little, she realized that it hadn't been a nightmare. Memories of what had taken place streamed in. She couldn't believe what she had done. She had blood on her hands without actual blood being on them. She was a murderer. She'd killed someone. She'd actually taken someone's life. Claudia was gone forever. Audra tried stifling her sobs. She didn't want anyone to hear her. The last thing she needed was to bring more attention to herself. What was going to happen now?

Probably best not to ask questions, just do whatever she was told. That's what she'd been doing since she'd arrived at the prison. Never would she ever have believed herself capable of stealing, but she'd lost her job. Money had always been tight, even when she was working but within a week of losing her job, her family had run out of food.

Audra's mom, Cherry, was already thin and sickly. Audra couldn't bear to sit back and watch her slowly die. She had to do something. At first, she'd tried picking up odd jobs, cleaning people's houses. It was enough to pay the odd bill and keep food in the house. It seemed to be working out… until it wasn't. After Cherry began to experience pain, they didn't have the money to seek medical care. There was no one to turn to so she took matters into her own hands and things went from bad to worse.

Audra entered the pharmacy, to casually browse among the aisles. Every so often, she'd pick up a package to read the back of it. She wanted painkillers, the strongest she could get. Her mother needed them badly but there was no way to pay for them. With two bottles in her hand, she glanced at the cashier who was busy taking a payment from an elderly woman. It was now or never. She slipped two bottles of pills into the pocket of her sweater.

The next thing Audra knew, someone had a firm grip on her arm. A member of The Agency had been behind her. Caught red-handed, she was given six months in The Cell. She'd been inside for a month when she learned that her mother had passed away. She knew she would never forgive herself for not being with her.

Obviously, Audra wasn't having a good time but the goal was to survive that torturous place and that was exactly what she was doing. If other people got hurt, it wasn't her fault. She was at the mercy of others. She wasn't going out of her way to destroy people but she'd do whatever was needed to make it through her sentence. Of course, she was upset about what had happened to Claudia. Audra had shared a room with her and the others. They'd gotten to know each other; she'd even considered Claudia to be a friend. As the tears welled again, she reminded herself it was The Agency's fault.

Audra had no idea what time it was. Trying to tease good memories to the surface to lull herself to sleep was a fruitless endeavor. She tossed and turned. At least her stomach was full. She also reminded herself that she was clean and comfortable for the first time in months. There was no point in thinking too much about the future. It was best to stay focused on the present.

26

Bev was surprised to find a note waiting when she got back to her room. It was from Captain Neal and it was sealed.

She quickly opened it with no idea how long it had been waiting. The last thing she needed was to irritate him. When she'd started working at The Cell, she'd figured out almost instantly that it was always best to keep on his good side. The note read:

Please come to the office at 18:00
CN

It was a good thing she'd decided to come back to her room instead of taking a walk in the shops. She took a quick look in the mirror to make sure she was presentable, then left for The Captain's office.

When Bev arrived, the door was closed, which was to be expected. She hated interrupting him, though. Someone else could be in the office with him. Never comfortable in this situation, she waited another moment before knocking, then waited.

"Come in."

He looked up as she entered. "Have a seat." He pointed toward the chair in front of her.

She sat down quickly.

"So, how are things going?"

Bev wondered how she was supposed to answer that. She watched people die and tended to the survivors. She watched people bet on lives for entertainment. His people made money and innocent people died. But she wasn't stupid. She knew there was only one answer. The only one he wanted to hear anyway.

"Good. I appreciate the help from the guards when they can offer it. Things have been going smoothly." Bev bobbed her head up and down to give herself a sense of confidence that she most certainly didn't feel.

"We need to make sure we keep the strong ones. Those that survive The Calling. Now if they're badly injured, they're not much use to us. Do you understand what I'm saying?" His eyes locked with hers. "Just a reminder."

Of course Bev knew exactly what he was saying. Whoever survived The Calling had to be in good shape. If their injuries were too severe, he had no use for them. In that case, they needed to be disposed of, quickly and efficiently. She had not only seen it done before, she was the one who did it. Those victims—those survivors—never woke up again. And they continued to haunt her.

"Of course, Captain," she replied quickly. She never second guessed what he was saying—at least, not in the moment. She would have time to think later. For now, she would listen as he continued to talk.

"I thought for some of the survivors, we'd put them in a separate block. Build another one. I'm calling it Rain for now. This would be a place for people to flourish and to hopefully increase the population. I need to make sure it's set up properly, though. This is one of my long-term projects. There's a lot of figuring and planning to be done first."

Bev nodded in agreement again even though she had no idea what his far-fetched plans entailed. "Sounds like a great idea."

"I knew you were a smart cookie. Good. Glad you agree."

Then he smiled and turned his back on her. She had been dismissed.

Bev couldn't describe the feeling but she sensed something was off. Something had shifted and it didn't feel good. It felt like The Captain might be going in another horrible direction. It was the part about increasing the population. She wondered how he planned to do that. She wasn't sure if people would be volunteering for this new project or if it would be another Calling situation where people didn't have a choice. Who knew what the outcome would be? The Captain seemed to relish the idea of playing with people's lives.

Over the last several months Bev had hoped the guards would get tired of The Callings and realize that The Agency should put a stop to them. Or maybe that other people would finally rise up and challenge them. But the opposite seemed to be happening. Two Callings had taken place in a matter of weeks.

Things were escalating. And not for the better.

27

Captain Neal loved the feeling that went through his body every time he entered the prison: pure power. As soon as he stepped inside that building, he felt the atmosphere change immediately. It was because of him and he never tired of it.

Guard Kep immediately spotted Captain Neal and ran over to be the first one to greet him. "Hey, Captain. Do you want me to make the rounds with you today? Or do you want someone else to go with you?"

"You can make the rounds with me, as usual. You can let me know if there's anything I should be aware of or any questions that need answering."

The Captain started walking. Kep scurried behind him.

"I'd like to see the women's floor first. There was a border brought here recently. I believe her name is Brie. I'd like to see the room she's in and see how she's adjusting."

"Whatever you like, Sir."

Moments later, they were at Room 10.

❈❈❈

As soon as Brie saw The Captain, she froze. She'd been in the middle of braiding Sally's hair. The other women instantly went silent with The

Captain's presence. They stood up. She followed their lead.

Brie wondered if it was normal for The Captain to inspect the rooms. She didn't believe for a minute that was the real reason he was at the prison. The women had mentioned before that The Captain came on site every so often, but nothing was said about his actually interacting with the borders. Brie knew it was best to keep quiet unless directly spoken to. From the moment she'd arrived at The Cell, that had been her plan: lay low, complete her sentence without incident, and avoid whatever The Calling was.

Brie wasn't sure how the latter was done. No one seemed to know. People in The Cell were too frightened to talk about it in case a guard might overhear. No one knew what the punishment would be. Would they be sent to The Basement, never to be seen again? Would more time be added to their sentence? Or would they be selected to participate in the next Calling? Brie couldn't take that chance. Her mouth had landed her here in the first place so she had to keep it tightly shut.

❖ ❖ ❖

Captain Neal remained silent. He always took great delight in making the borders wait. His eyes lingered over all four women.

He unconsciously tightened the smile on his face before he spoke. "Brie. How has your stay been so far?" He didn't need to ask which one of them was Brie. The memory of her defiance had surfaced once again the moment he laid eyes on her.

It took Brie a moment. "Okay."

His smile widened. She'd only been in The Cell for slightly more than a week and already her feistiness was starting to fade. The Captain had expected nothing less.

Captain Neal turned toward Kep. "Why is this one here?" He pointed at Nancy. He watched as Kep tapped his watch to pull up the information he was looking for.

"Her name is Nancy and she was given ninety days for kicking a male agent in the privates. It was unprovoked. She has completed almost one third of her sentence." Kep flipped his watch shut.

The Captain had assumed that Nancy would keep quiet unless

spoken to but he was wrong.

"It's not true!" she yelled.

Who the hell does she think she is? The Cell is supposed to make the borders complacent. Break them. She's been here long enough. This isn't good. I won't have her behaving like this. It doesn't make me look good.

"Excuse me? Do you have something you want to say to me?" When his eyes bore directly at her, he was expecting her to remain silent. Again, he was mistaken. This was a day filled with surprises.

"The Agent tried to feel me up. I told him to stop and he wouldn't."

"I hold my Agents to a high standard. I'm insulted that you would accuse them of such disgusting behavior. I'm sure if they wanted anything in that department, they wouldn't have trouble finding a willing participant. In fact, I can assure you of that."

He heard her mutter something in defiance. It was under her breath but he heard her. She'd had the disrespectful nerve to call him a liar.

"Kep? Add another ninety days to this woman's sentence for name calling and disrespecting authority. Her name's Nancy, right?"

"You can't do that!"

"I just did."

To his utter horror, she stepped forward and spat on him, the spittle landing on the front of his black shirt. His instinctive response was to reach out to grab her wrist.

"Kep. Take this one to The Basement. Cancel visitation for the others. It's time they learned their place. While they're in The Cell, they will obey me or there will be consequences."

"Yes, Sir."

28

Brie watched in horror alongside Sally and Mary as two other guards entered the room. Nancy pleaded with The Captain but he remained silent. Each of the new male guards grabbed one of Nancy's arms. When they attempted to move her outside the room into the hallway, she dropped her entire body.

Brie put a hand over her own mouth. Part of her did it to make sure she didn't say anything she might regret; the other part of her didn't want The Captain to see the small smile on her face. Of course, she didn't want Nancy going to The Basement. This was horrible. Rumor had it that once a border went to The Basement, there was a good chance they'd never be seen again. That might be only a rumor to create fear, but it worked. What had made her smile for that fraction of a moment was that Nancy was making it as hard as possible for the guards to make her go with them. *Good girl.*

Brie wanted to look away from the fear she saw in Nancy's eyes, but somehow knew it would be worse to turn away while the guards dragged the poor woman along the filthy floor.

Nancy continued to yell. "You can't do this to me. I haven't done anything wrong."

In a situation like this, the guards could do whatever they wanted and the borders were helpless to resist. If they talked back, if they asked too many questions, if they sat and did nothing at all, horrible things could happen. The rules for what was acceptable seemed extremely fluid. It was hard to believe, but things could always get worse.

The guards finally got Nancy onto her feet and into the hallway where Brie could still hear Nancy yelling, pleading her case, with no one replying.

Brie's eyes locked with Captain Neal's. He didn't say a word. He smiled then walked away.

***

Nancy was covered in filth by the time the guards threw her into The Basement. She'd struggled to get back up so she could walk down to The Basement, but it seemed she'd lost that chance the moment she'd tried to become dead weight. They dragged her, laughing and promising she was in for a grand old adventure. She knew her time in The Basement was going to be anything but a grand old adventure.

She was given a sheet, two metal buckets, paper towels and a few other things and immediately had the feeling this was going to be at the very least, ten times worse than the room she'd shared with the other women. There was no sleeping bag, just the sheet that looked like it might possibly have been white at one time. It had probably never been washed. Nancy shivered at that thought. She was in a whole new level of disgust here with no idea of how she might survive. Not only that, but time had been added to her sentence. She crossed her fingers in the hope she'd be in The Basement only briefly before being relocated back with the other women.

Nancy stayed on her feet for as long as she could but eventually she realized she needed to sit. All her energy had been wasted making the guards drag her down to The Basement. Both legs were scratched, and blood appeared in several spots. *Not good, not good at all.* The last thing she needed was to get an infection. She doubted the guards would allow a nurse to give her medical attention. Nancy couldn't believe she'd put herself in this position.

She reflected back to the day the guard tried to feel her up. Maybe she should've let him do what he wanted. Maybe none of this would have happened.

No. She'd always been one to stand up for herself. That was the one thing she'd always taken pride in. She had to stop playing the What If game because it didn't change a thing. It was dangerous mentally, a luxury she couldn't afford. She needed to stop that negative train in its tracks, now. If she didn't, she'd be stranded on that train until it sucked the last breath out of her. No. She wasn't done yet. This wasn't over.

But as this renewed sense of spirit filled her, a voice from close by whispered, "Welcome to your worst nightmare."

29

Something was wrong. Scotia could feel it. She'd never felt comfortable visiting The Cell but the atmosphere was different today. The visits with her sister were short and she was sure half the allotted time had already passed—she'd already been waiting in the visitation yard for several minutes—but she still couldn't find Brie.

She yelled her name again but all she heard was the chitter-chatter of prisoners and their loved ones.

Scotia turned to Ted who was at her side. "Something's wrong."

His jaw tightened. "We don't know that."

That's complete bullshit.

"Do you know any names of the women she's housed with?"

She couldn't believe the nonsense coming out of his mouth. "Yeah. She introduced them to me last time I was here, while we sipped on wine and ate cubed cheese with bamboo toothpicks." She gritted her teeth. Ted was amazing but most of the time, he annoyed the heck out of her.

A horn blast made Ted glance over at her. "What does that mean?"

"That means there are exactly two minutes left until the visitation is done and I'll have to wait another week to see her. The only thing would've kept her from seeing me today is if something bad happened." She reached her arm out to Ted's to steady herself. "Please. Not a Calling. What if there was a Calling?" She slid to the ground, Ted along with her to slow down her fall. If she let panic set in, she wouldn't be useful to anyone.

They sat in silence, Scotia listening to the others talk, then, taking in a deep breath, she asked the question she'd been dreading the answer to.

"Hey. Does anyone know if any borders were taken away?" She didn't want to mention the word Calling in case that set off a domino fall of panic. That's not what she wanted. She wanted—needed—a lead to what had prevented Brie from showing up.

Almost immediately, feet shuffled toward her and a female border appeared above her, looking off into the distance, and barely moving her lips, saying, "The Captain went into one of the rooms to check on a female border. Don't remember the name but she was a newer one. It wasn't her they took, but a girl in that same room. I heard someone say her name was Nancy. I don't know what happened but The Captain canceled visitation for everyone in that room and this girl, Nancy, was taken to The Basement." The female border shuffled away.

Another horn blast. Visitation was over.

Scotia now had even more questions. She found it strange that The Captain would be interested in a recent arrival. And what exactly had this woman named Nancy done to deserve a punishment as severe as what everyone said The Basement was?

This bit of welcomed gossip confirmed the rumor that The Basement *did* exist and *was* used as punishment but right now, her main worry was how her sister was holding up mentally and physically. Would she ever see Brie again?

30

It had been a few weeks since Valter had won The Calling. He couldn't really complain, he was being treated well. The food was good. Nothing was currently expected of him, although he was sure that could change any time now. He didn't believe for a second that The Agency would let him sit around doing nothing. There had to be a plan for him but he figured anything had to be better than serving time in The Cell. Then there was also the fact that he enjoyed his time with Bev. He knew it was wrong, but he liked her.

He considered himself to be one of the lucky ones. He'd only been sentenced to three months and that was because he'd fallen behind in paying his bills. The City of Kneel frowned upon not being able to support yourself. He was in his thirties and his first ever relationship had lasted only three months, but he was sure he'd been in love with her. However, it turned out that the only thing Tega was interested in was his money. Once his little nest egg was gone, so was she.

For weeks after Tega dumped him, Valter was in such a state of despair, he couldn't make it to his mechanic's job. After failing to show up for two weeks, he was fired. He stayed in bed and kept playing the relationship over and over in his mind, trying to figure out what had exactly gone wrong. Now it seemed silly but at the time, he thought if he could just figure it out, he might have a chance to fix everything.

The bills started piling up and at one point, Valter owed thousands of dollars. That was when the guards came to take him to The Cell. It wasn't like he could make any money while serving time, that part never made any sense to him. The only good thing was that now that he was finished his sentence, his debt was wiped clean. This was a good opportunity for him to start over. Before being sentenced to The Cell, he had seen Tega circling a woman named Scotia, which he thought was strange but whatever she did now was none of his business. He had only to worry about himself and that's exactly what he intended to do.

His recovery was going well but he knew that when he recovered, he would no longer see Bev. He enjoyed watching as she changed his bandages and liked the soothing sound of her voice. He had to remind himself that he was just part of her job, that she was probably nice to everyone, that he shouldn't let himself read too much into it.

Besides, he was a nobody, a nobody without a future, a nobody under the control of The Agency. Bev was a nurse who worked for them. They were on opposite sides. Nothing could ever happen between them.

Whenever Bev smiled, which wasn't as often as he would've liked, it gave him goosebumps. He often cracked little jokes, hoping it would make her laugh or smile. It was the one thing he looked forward to.

"Valter. You seem to be in the best of shape."

❄ ❄ ❄

She'd done this exact same thing countless times before so wondered, when she was alone at night, why Valter seemed different. She'd gone over their interactions more times than she'd like to admit. There was nothing out of place. She treated him with the same amount of respect and care as she did with the other survivors but somehow, Valter was different. She'd find herself going intentionally out of her way to get him the little things that seemed to matter, like his favorite food, pasta. She'd take the time to make sure everything was just right before she left his side and over the last week, she found herself making excuses to stop in and check on him even when it wasn't necessary.

During the first week, Audra had felt hopeful. She had her own space. The nurse, Bev, seemed as though she genuinely cared about her, always making sure that Audra was comfortable and had enough to eat and drink. For once, Audra didn't have to worry about when or where her next meal was coming from or if the guards would toss the food on the floor—or if the food was rotten and past its expiry date. When her food was brought to her now, it was always delicious and warm.

So now she allowed herself to start wondering what was going to happen next. It wouldn't stay like this forever. Something must come after The Calling. Although, since it was such a taboo topic, no one ever talked about it. All Audra hoped for was that she would never have to participate in it again. She had already felt a shift in her own identity. What she had done was something she would have to live with for the rest of her life. The good news was, she was a lot more resilient than she'd ever given herself credit for. The bad news was, never in a million years had she thought herself capable of hurting another human being let alone snuff their life out. Yet that's exactly what she'd done.

She tried reasoning with herself by playing devil's advocate. Had she really been given a choice when it came to The Calling? The rules were simple. Two people would compete. Audra had to be one of them and only one person would be allowed to live. She'd heard the expression "eat or be eaten" and this was exactly what it had boiled down to. She'd had a choice: live or die. Obviously, she didn't want to die. Although, if she were being honest, she had thought about suicide on more than one occasion. Maybe it would've been quicker and easier if she'd just let Claudia kill her.

There had been a price and she'd paid it. The question was, would she be willing to pay that price again to save herself? *It depends,* she thought. She'd made it this far so maybe she could go even further. She had to find a way to be able to still respect herself without losing her entire identity in the process.

Bev's eyes locked with Audra's, trying to send the message that she cared, beneath her words. "You'll be moving to the new area soon. You've done very well. You're physically healed. I'm not sure what else we can do for you here." She always hoped none of them would ask questions when she was spewing the rehearsed spiel because the truth was, she didn't have many answers. All she knew was that there was another area they were putting people in. These "chosen people" would be part of The Captain's Rain project. This would be where the healthy survivors were moved to.

She could feel Audra's eyes on her as she continued folding the newly washed towels and dishcloths.

"Why am I going there and what will happen to me next?"

"I'm not sure. I know you'll find it hard to believe but I don't really have the answers." Bev stopped what she was doing to direct her gaze at Audra. "I only know that The Captain wants you moved. Are you not happy to be moving on to the next chapter of your life?"

"I'd rather stay here knowing what to expect every day. Over there, I have no idea who's going to be there. Or what they are going to do me. I know it's a case of the knowing versus the not knowing. It scares the hell out of me."

"Fair enough. I don't blame you, girl." Bev turned her back to Audra again so her worry wouldn't be seen. She wondered if there was a way she could get Audra's move delayed by a week or two, like she had for Valter. But she wasn't sure if the girl had anything to worry about yet.

She also wanted to know what The Captain was up to, what this new project was really about.

31

Captain Neal toured Rain, the new wing on the top floor, currently under construction and would be for some time. The floor would contain twenty full-sized double rooms, five full-sized bathrooms, one common living area and a large kitchen with five stoves, five fridges, five sinks, five microwaves and five sets of kitchen tables and chairs. Each person granted a stay at Rain would have their own space. So far, it was mostly just the rooms that had been completed.

Merely thinking of all this gave The Captain goosebumps. Soon, he'd be able to transfer the chosen ones here.

"What's so important that you requested to see me?" he asked Blake, the guard with the piercing eyes. He wasn't in the mood to deal with any nonsense today.

"It's the girl you sent down to The Basement, Sir. Nancy. She refuses to eat. We drop the food off, we go back later for the dishes and it looks like she hasn't touched anything." Blake cleared his throat. "We just wanted to make sure you were aware. Sir."

Captain Neal knew what Blake wanted. He wanted direction on how to deal with the girl. For a minor thing, the guards looked after it themselves; they didn't bother him with it. He believed this was the first time any guard had come to him because one of the idiot borders was refusing to eat. Usually, they were demanding more food, or more water, or toiletry items—which, of course, he always denied because The Basement was meant to be extra punishment.

"Well, if she's refusing to eat, don't give her any food and see what happens. Borders can be ungrateful sometimes. They don't realize how good they have it not having to worry when their next meal is going to come. We are generous enough to provide it to them free of charge. If she's unable to see that, perhaps she needs time to reflect. A week? Yes. Bring her a single glass of water in the morning during food rounds. I'm sure if you do that, it'll be only a matter of days before she realizes how ungrateful she is and will have a change of heart."

Blake nodded, turned and left.

❧ ❧ ❧

Nancy heard what she was sure was a male voice whispering at her. It was difficult to know for sure. It was dark and you weren't supposed to move around in The Basement. Everyone had their own spot.

The male cleared his throat. "I don't know why you're refusing to eat. You're being difficult. They don't like that. All our actions have consequences. If that weren't the case, we wouldn't be down here."

"It isn't like the food's any good. I'm not missing out on anything." She was determined to stand her ground. In this environment, there weren't many things she had control over, but accepting food was one of them.

Nancy's reply was met with fresh silence but only for a moment. "Do you know what month it is by chance?"

"It's August. I arrived a few weeks ago. How long have you been here?"

"Since last year," he said. "I think it was December. There was snow on the ground."

"How long have you been in The Basement? Since December?" Nancy couldn't believe he'd been here that long. She also wondered what he'd done to land himself in the same position she now found herself in.

"The day I arrived, they took me to The Basement right away. They were upset." The voice chuckled.

"They must have been if they put you here right away." Nancy figured he wouldn't answer but it was worth a shot. "What did you do anyway?"

"One of the Agents tried to mess with Lily. My wife. We were at the market. I left her for two seconds to grab some lettuce at the vegetable stall. She was looking around for the perfect loaf of bread. Next thing I knew, she was yelling at somebody to leave her alone, that she was with her husband. I ran right over to where I left her but she wasn't there. Then I spotted her in an alley with a guy. An Agent. Her pants were halfway down and he was pulling on her shirt. I lost it. I ran for him and started swinging and I kept swinging." The voice chuckled again. "The Agent had to be hospitalized. I don't know for how long and I still don't care if he lived or died. At the time, it felt great pounding him, but now I'm here. Being in silence all the time is hard. In the City, you get to hate the sound of drones spying on you all the time, but if you spend enough time in The Basement, you'll find yourself wishing you could."

She decided to ask him, "What's your name and how long is your sentence?"

It was quiet for so long she thought she wasn't going to get an answer. She figured she should let it go for now, ask again another time.

Then, "I have no idea." His voice was flat.

"It says on your cert how long you're here. I was originally here for ninety days. I served half of that and now they've added another ninety days."

"I remember when they read out my cert..."

"OK. So the length of the sentence... They would've read that to you at the same time."

"That's the thing," he said. "The cert didn't say how many days I was to be here. It said TBD. When I asked the guard what that meant, he said it meant The Agency could keep me for however long they wanted. That's when I knew I was never getting out of here. Amos. My name's Amos, by the way."

Nancy was speechless. She'd never heard of someone being sent here without an actual sentence. It didn't seem right. But neither did a lot of things. She wondered how many other women had been attacked.

After another long silence, the conversation started up again. "I haven't seen Lily since the day it happened. Because I'm in The Basement, they won't let me see her. Maybe she doesn't even know I'm alive. I don't know if she's okay. I pray every day for the strength to carry on. That's the reason I make sure to eat every day, too. To have the strength to make it through. I hope some day I'll have a chance to hold her in my arms again."

Hearing his words made Nancy think twice about her refusal to eat. Tomorrow, when the food trays came around, she'd eat. Maybe there was a way she could help Amos find out if his wife was doing okay, and get word to her that he was still alive, that he was doing okay.

Nancy wasn't sure if "doing okay" was the right phrase to describe his condition, but he was managing. In a place like this, that definitely counted for something. As long as he was alive, there was hope. That was all it took: one ounce of hope and the human spirit would rise again.

❀ ❀ ❀

Nancy waited patiently while the guards dropped off food for the others. She was actually looking forward to breakfast this morning. She hadn't eaten in a few days. Today was different though. She felt like she now had another purpose, something besides herself. She didn't have any family waiting for her on the outside. No one.

Of course, back in the room, she'd gotten to know the other women: Mary, Sally and Brie. She cared if something happened to them, but somehow, after chatting with Amos, his story mattered more. She wanted to help him write a better ending.

Nancy took notice when the guard carrying the food trays walked right by her. "Hey, where's my food?"

He stopped and smiled at her.

She didn't like the way he was looking at her.

"Oh," he said. "I nearly forgot. Thanks for the reminder." He handed her a small plastic cup of water then walked away.

"What about my food?"

"You didn't want it so my orders are no food for you."

"For how long?" This wasn't good. No. She needed to keep up her strength. She had to get back to her room alive and strong. Maybe the other women would be able to help her with Amos and Lily.

The guard called back. "Sorry. Your choice."

She shrunk onto the cold, hard, concrete floor. The guard wasn't going to tell her anything.

"No food," whispered Amos. "This can't be good."

"My thoughts exactly."

Nancy hoped it was only for a day or two. It had already been two days since she'd eaten anything. She was exhausted. She wondered how long a person could go without food.

32

It was visitation day. Brie was looking forward to having her sister visit her. It was hard to believe she'd already been in The Cell for three weeks—and even harder to believe that, so far, her time had been manageable.

As soon as they were let outside, she ran to where she and Scotia had visited the last time. It didn't take long for her to spot Scotia and for Scotia to spot her.

Scotia started walking faster and Ted wasn't far behind. Brie motioned for her to get closer and she did, trying to talk to each other, share news, at the same time.

Brie held up her hand. She had to speak first. "They took our roommate, Nancy, and they put her downstairs. Because she went downstairs and because it was our room, our visits were canceled. I swear I'm okay, Sosh."

Brie wanted to make sure she didn't use the word basement. She thought it safer to say "downstairs," knowing her sister would pick up on it.

Sure enough, she did, nodding her head slightly and making direct eye contact with Brie.

Good. She understands. Brie didn't want to use up any more time talking about Nancy. She was afraid someone would eavesdrop and it would get back to the guards. Knowing *her* luck, she'd get more time added to her sentence. She needed to keep low, like she'd been doing. Her method had worked so far.

Ted tried to get a few words in. "We're thinking of you all the time. Let us know if there's anything we can do."

Brie had to stifle a laugh. He sounded so casual. She knew he didn't mean it like that, but in reality, he wasn't able to do a single thing.

"Sosh, we have to change things."

Just then, the blast of the horn, the two minute warning, filled the air.

Their eyes connected. Scotia put her right index finger to her lips for a fraction of a section. Brie understood. Scotia wanted her to stop her line of conversation.

Three long blares from the horn made Brie jump. Scotia and Ted exchanged glances with each other and then with her. Everyone stared at everyone else, then looked around. Brie had no idea what those blares meant. It was the first time they'd heard three blares in a row.

Brie and the others looked in the direction of the doors they'd used to get into the yard for visitation. They could see two guards. It appeared as though they had two borders with them. The crowd grew silent.

Over the loudspeaker, an announcement declared: "Sentence completed."

Brie couldn't believe it. The borders had completed their sentence and were being released. She wasn't sure how often it happened. At least that part wasn't a myth. This gave her a renewed sense of hope. Maybe The Agency really would let her go when her time was up.

❈ ❈ ❈

Bev hadn't slept well. She'd been up part of the night, thinking about the new place, Rain, and also about Valter. Maybe she wouldn't be able to see him if he were officially moved to the new area. She wasn't sure how she felt about that. It was probably a good thing though. She wasn't sure if he was being extra nice to her because he knew she was the one who had control over his medication and the many other things he needed during his stay, or if there was something more to it. She tried brushing the feeling off. If there was anything more to it, it didn't really matter. It wasn't as though anything could ever happen between them. She was reading too much into things. She needed to stop doing that and focus on getting sleep so she could make it through another demanding day.

She walked up closer to Valter with the intention of doing nothing more than talk to him. Somehow, she managed to lose her balance and would have fallen had he not caught her. He held her for a moment. She wasn't sure what to say except, "Sorry."

"Are you okay?" He was still holding her. She could feel him and it felt good. She closed her eyes. He still didn't let go. Together they stood as though frozen. He caressed her back. She couldn't remember the last time she'd felt... Felt what? Felt the need to step away from him? The thing was, though, she didn't want to. She'd enjoyed his touch, even though he was probably just being polite. Bev decided she would count to five and then take a step back. *One, two, three...* And the next thing she knew, his lips were on hers.

His lips felt amazing. She didn't want to pull away from him but she opened her eyes, pushed him slightly then quickly glanced around.

"I'm sorry," he said.

"I'm not." Bev hoped there hadn't been any witnesses.

Her eyes connected with his. He glanced away to check for witnesses then leaned in again to kiss her.

This time it was different. He slipped his tongue into her mouth and she instantly felt a warm rush, a pleasant sensation throughout her body. She pulled away, not because she wanted to, but because she had no idea what would happen to them if they were caught.

Bev wasn't sure what to say. Maybe it was better to pretend nothing had happened. It had felt wonderful. He was good looking. She loved his eyes and the sound of his voice. His lips had felt fantastic on hers. But it was over.

"I don't want to stop this... How I feel," Valter whispered.

Bev didn't know what so say so she walked out of the room.

✽ ✽ ✽

Later that night, Bev thought about Valter's touch, his lips, his eyes and how she'd felt when he kissed her. It had been magical. That night was the first time she'd slept through the night, and had felt rested on waking up in the morning. She had no idea how it might happen but she wanted to see where things led with him. If that was something he was open to. Maybe it was time she took a leap of faith and started listening to her intuition. She was tired of following everyone else's orders and always being the good girl. What all that hard work had given her was nothing but heartache. The job made her feel useful, yes. She enjoyed working with the borders, yes. She despised the reason she had to attend to them, but the comfort she could provide brought her joy. For years, she hadn't let herself hope for anything. Maybe, maybe it was time for something else. She knew if things didn't work out, there'd be consequences. That was something she definitely had to be aware of at all times.

Bev decided it might be best if she let Valter make the next move. See what he wanted. Had it perhaps been a weak moment? Or had he hoped he could get something out of her. She had no idea why he'd kissed her, but there was a sliver of hope that what had taken place was genuine. They could talk about it next time she saw him. For now, she would enjoy replaying the memory of what had taken place.

✽ ✽ ✽

Valter had no idea what he must have been thinking when he'd leaned forward and kissed Bev. It hadn't been planned. Well… If he were being honest with himself, maybe it had been planned. Subconsciously. He'd lost count as to how many times he'd thought about kissing her.

At first he'd liked her because she was nice to him. He knew it was her job as a nurse to look after everyone. Even though she seemed to be especially nice to him, he hadn't really thought anything of it. She just seemed like an amazing person who enjoyed her job and went above and beyond to make sure everyone was okay.

As time went on, though, he started feeling better and better. A week after she'd stopped by more than a dozen times to check on him, he knew his feelings for her had changed. That was when he really started to fall for her.

The more Valter tried not to think about her, the more he did. It was pointless. Thinking about Bev helped him with his recovery and that was what kept him going. He had thought about expressing how he felt to see if she felt the same. He wasn't sure how that conversation would go. He had replayed a scene over and over in his mind, but no matter what, it didn't seem genuine. He kept putting it off and then today, they had kissed. Now the big question was: what would it be like when he saw her next? Would it be uncomfortable? He wasn't sure how Bev felt but he was sure he couldn't sit back and pretend nothing had happened. He wanted to kiss her again and again. He wanted more. But at the same time, he wasn't sure why she'd want anything to do with him. She was a nurse who worked for The Agency. He was a border with no idea what his future held.

He was frustrated. He'd finally met someone and he never thought that would happen. He'd met someone who seemed to, at least for the moment, be interested in him as well. Things might end before they even got started. It was frustrating. Was there was a way he could figure something out? In his heart, he felt that the chances were really slim, but it would still be worth trying, for many reasons. Bev had been the reason he'd been able to keep going.

The more he thought about his knowledge of The Calling, the more questions he had. He'd survived and that meant he was golden, untouchable. At least that's what the rumor was. That's what the guard had told him when he'd been declared the winner. The truth? Valter didn't know.

Maybe what he'd been told was a lie. Borders were always being told things that weren't true. During his recovery, the more he thought about it, the more confused he became. In his room, before The Calling, he'd at least known what to expect. Now that The Calling was over, he wasn't sure. During the first few days following The Calling, he wished he could fall asleep and never wake up. Now, thinking about that time in his life, he was ashamed for those feelings. He should have been grateful for what he did have. Like Bev.

It was Bev who encouraged him, who tried to make him comfortable. She'd done this by keeping him physically well and making sure he had everything he needed. And, he realized now, she'd also done this by spending more time with him after rounds. He soon realized there was no way Bev was supposed to stay with patients for more than a few minutes. He had become special to her, too. Had he put her in danger by kissing her? Had anyone seen them? Now he was worried.

33

Ted couldn't believe what his cousin, Badger, had just disclosed to him. The stakes were high. He had to be certain. "Are you sure?"

Badger stood there with his arms crossed against his chest to make it look like he was doing something official, not disclosing information that he shouldn't be. "I'm telling you, The Captain asked to gather a file with a few people he wanted to um... 'discuss things with.' That's all I can say. I shouldn't be telling you any of this. I'm really sticking my neck out here."

"And Brie's name is on that list?"

"Yes. I remembered you have a thing for Scotia, and you sometimes talk about her sister. As soon as I heard the name Brie, I knew it was probably her. I have zero control over anything else but I thought I'd pass this on. Maybe you can do something before it's too late."

Ted knew he needed to back off and give Badger some credit. If he kept pressuring him, the next time any important information came up, there was no way Badger would share it. Ted needed to stay on Badger's good side.

"I want you to know how much I appreciate this information, Badger. I owe you one."

"I only told you because you're the only family I have left. Even if we're just cousins." Badger walked away and out of the coffee shop.

Ted quickly finished his coffee. He had to get in touch with Scotia as soon as he could. He was reluctant to, but figured he didn't really have a choice. If something happened to Brie and he'd been sitting on this information the whole time, it would blow up in his face. He'd been friends with the family for years and had thought of Brie as a sister. He had a feeling things were about to change, and not in a good way.

✻ ✻ ✻

Scotia tried to be gentle at first but Tega wasn't taking no for an answer. They had shared another intimate kiss. This time, it felt different for Scotia. The first kiss they shared had been enjoyable, even exciting, but they'd shared more kisses since then and each time, her feelings had been less so. The kiss they had just shared had really made Scotia uncomfortable.

Tega traced her finger down the front of Scotia's chest which made Scotia grab Tega's hand—gently, though—and move it away while shaking her head. She wasn't interested.

"Come on, lighten up."

"I don't want to. I think we should go back to the way we were before." She had to let her know she was serious, that she wasn't going to back down.

"What do you mean like before? You're not making sense."

"I'm not interested in being anything more than friends, Tega. I'm sorry. This just isn't working out. I'm not ready for a relationship."

Scotia was trying to be as gentle as possible. She'd heard rumors about how needy and unpleasant Tega could be when she didn't get her own way. The last thing Scotia wanted was to create a problem. She needed to focus on Brie, figure out what to do about The Agency. Things had changed. A specialty building was being erected and the gossip about what it might be used for was not positive.

"No, Scotia. That's not true and you know it. You're just worried about Brie. I get it. But you have to learn to relax. You're allowed to have your own life. Not everything has to revolve around Brie. I know she's your sister, but you deserve to be happy." Tega put her hand over Scotia's.

Scotia quickly pulled it away and immediately rose to her feet. Tega wasn't getting it. Scotia had to put an end to it. She'd never been with a woman. At first, when Tega had showed interest in her, she thought maybe there was something there, but as they spent more time together, she realized it had only been a crush, a passing feeling. Scotia didn't want anything more to happen between them. They hadn't been intimate, just hand holding and a couple of kisses but that had been enough. If Scotia were really attracted and interested in that special way, she would have had butterflies in her stomach.

"I want you to leave and I think we should spend some time apart."

"You're just upset over Brie. Give it some time and you'll come around."

As Tega reached the door, a knock made her turn back to look at Scotia with questioning eyes.

It was Ted and he didn't skip a beat. "Oh. So this is why you were trying to throw me out so quickly. Everything makes sense now. Toss me aside and move on quick."

"What? That's not what this is about and you know it." Scotia held the door open, figuring it was the best way to sweep a visibly angry Tega out of the apartment. To Tega she said, "I told you how I feel. You need to respect that."

"You'll regret this." Tega growled as she left.

While closing the door behind her, Scotia told Ted, "Don't ask." She wasn't in the mood to talk about anything or especially explain what had just happened.

"I came to see you because I have information regarding Brie. That's all."

"What? Spit it out."

"Badger. My cousin. He works at The Cell and—"

"What? Why are you just telling me this now? He could've been keeping an eye on Brie." Scotia couldn't help it, she was irritated. More than irritated and she knew her face showed it.

"Badger provides information to The Captain at the prison when he requests it. He's been trying to keep his head down and only do as he's told. Or asked. I don't know exactly what's going on, but I get the feeling something bad might be happening to Brie soon."

"Tell me exactly what he told you and don't leave anything out."

They moved to the couch, sat down, and Ted proceeded to tell her everything he knew.

34

Bev entered the room to see Valter lying there on his bed. He was awake and appeared to be deep in thought. She smiled as she walked toward him and he quickly turned toward the sound of her footsteps and immediately smiled when he saw who it was.

"Good morning, and how are we feeling?" She couldn't help it. She leaned in and kissed him—passionately—then pulled away. "I'm not sure where this is going."

"I want this. I want you," said Valter. "I can't stop thinking about you. When I first got here, of course I looked forward to seeing you because you were the only one able to take my pain away. But after the first few days, things changed."

Bev couldn't help it. The moment her lips had touched his, it was instant goosebumps. Kissing him felt good and right. She checked the hallway and saw that the coast was clear. She didn't think anyone else would come by anytime soon.

She sat on the edge of the bed. Valter sat up straight, put his hand over hers, and held it. She didn't remember the last time she'd felt this happy. Whatever this was, she wanted more. She closed her eyes as Valter raised his hand to caress the side of her face. His touch felt incredible. She wanted and needed more.

Before she realized what she was doing, she slid her hand down his chest to hover near the waistline of his pajama bottoms. Their eyes locked. At first, she hesitated, but felt the gentle nudge of his hand directing hers. Was she really going to do this? Yes, she was. Her right hand was now inside his pajamas and he was hard. As she stroked him, he moaned quietly.

❀ ❀ ❀

The Captain wanted to check in to see how some of the winners from The Calling were doing. He'd been told that the last two, Valter and Audra, were doing well and would soon be ready to be moved to the new location. He couldn't afford to let anything to go wrong. He'd visit each of them personally. He was especially interested in the woman, Audra. She seemed quite feisty and he was currently looking for a new companion.

First, though, he'd stop in to see Valter. That way, if Audra seemed interesting, he'd have more time to spend with her. He'd always been efficient with his time-management skills.

He checked his wrist device and noted that Valter was in Room 3. As he was passing the second room, which was empty, he paused, thinking he heard a strange noise. He picked up his pace and entered Room 3.

His footsteps had no doubt been heard by Bev because the moment he entered the room, she immediately stood up and distanced herself from the bed. But it was too late. It was obvious to him, that something intimate had been going on between her and Valter. He couldn't believe that Bev, who'd been by his side and had been so loyal to him, would dare do anything like this. If she were capable of this, what else she might she have done?

"What on earth is going on here, Bev?"

She stood staring at the floor.

"I want an explanation and I want it now." He waited but she didn't move. Nothing. "Well? What do you have to say for yourself?"

"I care about him."

"What? He was in The Calling. What do you mean you care about him? You can't be involved with any of these people and you know why. You are to do your job and your job is whatever I tell you to do, and that's it.

"Sir... Is there anything I can do? I need to be with him."

"Obviously, I can no longer trust you. Maybe this one should be taken to The Basement."

Valter had remained silent until then. "Not The Basement. I won The Calling fair and square. I'm a free man. You can't do this to me."

The Captain laughed. "I can do whatever I want and there's nothing you can do to stop me."

He pulled Bev out of the room with him.

❋ ❋ ❋

Scotia had gone back and forth on the idea she had in her head. It would be risky, but it was starting to look like it was the only choice. They needed to get Brie out of the prison. It was risking a lot, she knew, but at this point, the alternative was death. Brie was going to be forced to participate in The Calling at any moment. Scotia had to decide, and fast, and this was all she had.

❋ ❋ ❋

Brie knew Kep wanted to get on her good side, that he probably thought if he passed on information to her, she might learn to trust him.

He stepped toward her with the breakfast tray and spoke quietly. "I'm sorry. About Nancy. Your roommate. She didn't make it."

"What?" Brie wanted to scream out a hundred questions but she knew Kep was already taking a risk by sharing even this much.

"She passed away last night. I can't get into it but she's gone and I'm sorry." He turned and walked away.

She wanted to stop him but didn't dare put both of them in jeopardy.

❋ ❋ ❋

As soon as Kep left, Mary and Sally gathered around Brie.

"Did I hear right?" asked Mary. "I can't believe it. How can she be gone? Just like that?"

"We need to do something," said Brie. "They can't keep getting away with this. Punishing us over and over again. No matter what we do, they're never going to be happy. They're constantly taking things away."

Tears were forming in Mary's eyes. "I know what they're doing isn't right but I don't think there's anything we can really do."

"Well, I don't know about you," said Brie. "But I'm not going to sit around waiting until they drag me out to participate in their evil game. That's something people don't come back from. Think about it. We know the game exists. We know they take two people away for it each time. We know there's a winner and there's a loser but we don't really know what that means. If we leave this room before our sentence is over, we never come back."

"What can we do?" said Sally. "Nothing. They're in control."

"I'm not going to sit back and wait. I want to get out of here alive."

"And exactly how are you going to do that?" Mary's tears were halfway down her cheeks.

"I don't know yet. I just know I'm not going to sit back and wait. I don't want whatever happened to Nancy to happen to me." She glanced around her, pointing at the dark, dirty walls. "I want to get out of this place. I want things to change. I'm tired of living like this. The only way things will change is if we learn to stick together and stand up for ourselves."

She hoped her words would motivate and inspire the other two.

Apparently not, though, because neither spoke up.

35

It was almost forty-four hours since Valter had last seen Bev. He was worried. He wondered if The Captain had punished her. He wondered *if* The Captain was going to punish her and if so, how. It was hard to imagine a life without her. He didn't want that to happen. He felt sick just thinking about it.

He needed to find a way to see her again. He'd felt strong and fully recovered for nearly a week now. He'd been downplaying how he felt physically so he could continue to spend as much time as he could with her, and there was also the fear of not knowing what The Agency expected of him once he was fit and healthy. He knew he had the energy to find her, but he had no idea where to begin. Not to mention, he couldn't just go off on some half-baked adventure. He had to be smart, knowing that if he got caught, the consequences would be brutal. The Agency was capable of murder. After all, that's exactly what The Calling was about: killing people purely for profit and entertainment.

Captain Neal had just been informed that the female border, Nancy, whom he'd ordered into The Basement for spitting on him, hadn't made it. She'd passed away. It was unfortunate, but he didn't really care.

Obviously, this meant she wasn't strong enough to be a candidate for his plan of having a strong city. He wanted his city, Kneel, to be at its peak. The only way to ensure this was to have strong people everywhere.

Nancy's death could stir up trouble. That was worrisome. Catching the person he'd thought was his *faithful* nurse, Bev, with that man, Valter, had created unacceptable feelings inside him. Was he losing control? He could NOT let that happen! He needed to nip both potentially big problems in the bud before any more developed.

Knowing he had to act quickly, he decided to make a bold move and added Brie's name to the list for The Calling. He didn't care who she went up against. He hoped she wouldn't survive but if she did, he'd deal with it when the time came. First things first. It was time for Brie to participate in The Calling.

Next, he had to do something about Valter. Since it was clear that Bev had romantic feelings for him, Captain Neal could use this to his advantage. He figured he could probably get Bev to do absolutely anything he wanted to keep her precious Valter safe. She would do it or else he'd have Valter taken care of and that would be the end of that. He'd known Bev for a couple of years and couldn't believe she would have fallen for one of *them*. It disgusted him. He'd always respected her and at one point, even had a crush on her and had seriously thought of pursuing it. He thought they got along well, that perhaps their friendship would develop into something more. But after catching her with that man, he wanted nothing more to do with her. He'd lost all respect. She'd crossed a line. He would make her pay.

Of course, he wouldn't do anything right away. He wanted to catch her off guard. If he let time pass, she'd no doubt believe that everything was fine. That's when he would make his move. That part, he would figure out soon enough.

Captain Neal spoke into his watch: "Badger. I just want to confirm that Brie is on the list. I want her watched carefully. In fact, I want the next Calling done within the next forty-eight hours. Let me know when we're ready to start. I want to be there. I need to be there."

Badger's voice came through clearly. "Whatever you need, Captain.

I also… sorry… need you to know that the drones aren't working. I have them all in my office right now. I'll have to work on them. Individually. Shouldn't take too long."

That's what Captain Neal needed, more workers like Badger. It was now a done deal. Brie's time was up. "Sounds good. Keep me posted about the drones."

❈ ❈ ❈

Bev had known it was only a matter of time before she'd be called to The Captain's office so she'd hatched a plan. Never in her wildest dreams had she thought herself ever capable of something like it but reminded herself that it wasn't on her. The Captain had pushed her and it was her time to push back. And she would, drastically.

The day after she'd been caught with Valter, she'd visited the pharmacy—after hours to ensure no one would be around. She still had the key from when she'd worked there as an assistant, helping the pharmacist dole out the various medications. And now, all that knowledge was going to come in handy.

She took only slightly more than she needed. She didn't want the pharmacist to notice anything was off and then alert The Agency before she had a chance to follow through with her plan. It was imperative that no one else knew, or was involved. Whatever happened, the blame would be on her and on her alone. If her plan failed, or if anyone found out, the consequences would be The Cell or death. She didn't want anyone else to get in trouble for what she was about to do.

Bev was aware of the what and the why of her plan. There were two reasons: she wanted to be with the love of her life; and she wanted to bring about change. The only way both of those could happen was if Captain Neal was out of the picture. She'd waited long enough and could no longer stand by feeling useless. She knew that at any moment The Captain might do something to Valter. That was just who he was. There was no way The Captain would let them hold hands and skip off into the sunset toward their happily ever after.

The death concoction was in a small pouch that could easily be concealed in the palm of her hand, and as the hours ticked by, she practiced her plan over and over. She figured she had a fifty-fifty chance of actually pulling this off.

She slowly looked around her room. This could be the last time she would ever see it because The Captain had sent word that she was to meet him in his office tonight at 7:00 PM. It was now or never. She wished she could stop shaking. She had to believe in what she was doing. It was for the greater good—not only for her, but for everyone. It was time for the dissection and it looked like it was up to her to do it. Challenge accepted.

❀ ❀ ❀

Brie knew something was wrong before the guards even stepped into the room. She knew by the insistent chatter that had started brewing a couple of hours earlier. Brie knew even from her so-far brief experience in prison that this could only mean one thing: something bad was about to happen. Any second now.

"Brie, step forward."

She didn't move. Her feet felt like they were frozen to the floor. The guards didn't make a lot of social calls. If they wanted her for something, it wouldn't be for something good. The only reason she could think of was The Calling. Was her biggest fear about to come true?

"It's The Calling, isn't it? Just tell me." That was all she said but what she really wanted was to start spitting out a variety of profanities. She managed to control herself, deciding it was best to say as little as possible, needing to keep an eye on everything that was happening. Maybe she could somehow talk her way out of whatever was about to happen. Or find an advantage. Or make a run for it or, or, or... All she knew for sure was, she wasn't going to sit back and do nothing. She had to put up a fight.

"Let's go. You too, Mary."

Brie saw the look in Mary's eyes. *As if they would put us together!*

Mary didn't say a word. She just let the guards grab her.

36

Scotia walked as fast as she could. She wanted to run but was afraid that would draw attention. Ted was behind her. She thought it strange that the drones weren't hovering around as always. Had The Captain changed his mind, or…? No. Something was going on. She wasn't sure what; she didn't have time to figure it out; she just had to go rescue her sister.

"Tell me again what your plan is," demanded Ted. "Oh, right. You don't have one."

"I told you before, if you don't want to be a part of this, then stay home. In fact, didn't I tell you it was in your best interests to do just that? And yet, here you are?"

"I want to help," he said. "I just need to know what we're going to be doing when we get there. We can't just show up, knock on the door and expect them to hand over your sister. That's not going to happen."

"Just follow me and keep quiet. I don't want anyone to hear us or, worse, follow us to see what we're doing."

"Okay. You're the boss," he said. "No matter what I say anyway, there's no way you're going to turn back now." Then he muttered, "My life will never be the same after this."

"Shh. Quiet."

"Okay. Okay."

✤ ✤ ✤

Valter had imagined a variety of scenarios he might have ended up in after being caught with Bev. The rumored Basement had crossed his mind but he could never have dreamed it would be this bad.

He was now in the cold, damp, dark Basement. Already, he'd lost track of time but figured it had been about three hours. When he'd first arrived, he sat quietly to take in the surroundings.

Life in The Basement didn't look promising but he thought there might be a chance he could make it. That was until he started talking to another prisoner, Amos. After he heard Amos's story, he knew this would be the last stop. His life was probably over. He'd most likely die in The Basement. He learned that Amos hadn't done anything but had been in The Basement since forever, and that Nancy had died here, slowly and painfully.

Consequently, Valter was sure it was over for him, that there was no way he'd see the light of day again. Strangely enough, that was not the thought that bothered him the most. He needed Bev. He needed her just as much as he needed oxygen. He couldn't live without either. Maybe it was better this way. If they couldn't be together, he didn't want to be around anymore anyway. Bev would have told him to stop with the negative thoughts, to stop letting his mind go in such a dark direction. As long as Bev was still around, he had to keep fighting so they'd have a chance to be together. Loving and being loved in this world was a lot more than some people had. He was one of the lucky ones. He had experienced love.

If he and Amos kept talking, they might be able to come up with an escape plan. Surely, Amos would be interested in that. But, whatever plan they might be able to come up with, had to happen soon. If there was one thing he was sure of, time was running out. From past experiences, he knew he should always trust his gut.

✤ ✤ ✤

Bev stood outside The Captain's office door. In her hand, she held the mixture that would take care of him for good. She didn't know what would happen after that, but she would take one step at a time. *First step: Knock on the door.*

She knocked. She waited for The Captain's voice to give her permission to enter his office. He did. She entered.

"Thanks for coming."

Tread carefully. If you back out, Valter will be gone forever. And whatever The Captain has in store for you will be almost as bad as the heartbreak of that. The coveted position she'd enjoyed for years was already slipping away and would soon be completely demolished.

"I wanted to talk to you about your behavior with the survivor, the prison guy."

"His name is Valter."

The Captain waved his hand as though the name of the person she was risking everything for wasn't important. She'd expected nothing less from him; he hadn't made it to where he was by caring about others.

Second step. Bev made her move. "Shall I pour you a coffee?"

He smiled his usual power smile at her. "That would be nice."

At his coffee machine, her back was toward him. She turned her head slowly over her left shoulder to see him flipping some sort of big charted diagrams, no doubt blueprints for more of his horrible torture buildings, buildings to hide things in that he didn't want others to see. She turned forward again, and listening to the shuffling paper, she poured coffee into the mug. Quickly, she emptied the little packet in her palm and swirled it into the coffee with a spoon. It dissolved in seconds.

"The usual cream and sugar?"

"Yes."

She added everything he wanted, then giving it an extra stir, she mouthed a prayer that the coffee would taste fine, that he'd drink it, and that he'd still want her to be in the office. She didn't want to have to come up with reasons to hang around, waiting.

"Feel free to make yourself a cup."

This was good. She would, and she'd try her best to keep him talking until the poison took effect, then worry about that when it happened.

Bev sat down with her coffee and tried not to stare at him as he took the first sip. She wondered how much of it he'd have to drink. She hoped not much. She wanted this over with as soon as possible.

She couldn't believe she'd actually gone this far. There was no going back out now. No. That wasn't true. She could tell him what she'd done. She could "accidentally" knock over his coffee. She could stop it. *No. Stand your ground. See it through.*

"I think it's time we talked about that fella," said The Captain, setting his mug aside. "The one I caught you with." He glared at her, his eyes full of disgust. At least they had that in common. She felt the same way about The Captain. She couldn't believe how he constantly played with other people's lives. Did he believe he was God?

"Sir?" Bev had no idea what she could say that would be acceptable, but she was going to keep him in conversation, any conversation, somehow.

The Captain smiled that smile again. "The temptation has been removed. He'll not be a problem for you anymore." He reached for his coffee.

She moved toward the edge of her seat. "I'm not sure I follow you, Sir."

"I had that fellow moved. You won't be seeing him again." He took a big sip from the mug.

"I guess that's what we deserve, but are you sure?" She had to keep playing the part, make sure it looked like she was agreeing to whatever decisions had been made.

"Oh, I'm positive." He held the mug up. "This is good. Well done, Bev. Well done." He set the mug down again. "He's in The Basement. He won't last long there. They never do. Especially since he was a survivor."

She wanted to stand up and slap the smirk off his damned face. *Stay calm or this is going to blow up in your face. We're close. Feel it. Hang in there a little while longer.*

He sipped again.

Drink up, Drink up. How much longer does Valter have?

"There won't be any problem from me," she assured him, bowing her head in mock subservience.

"Good." Another sip. He set it down and Bev could see that his coffee was half gone. "Now. We need to move on to the next the step."

"And what's that?" She made eye contact with him, wanting to see if she could detect any symptoms of poisoning yet.

"We'll be matching up the people who'll be residing in Rain with others." He picked up his mug, took several gulps, set it down. "I want to increase the population. The numbers need to increase, not decrease."

"How do you propose we—?" That was as far as she got.

The Captain clutched his chest. He motioned at her with his other arm. Was he hoping she'd jump off her chair? Rush to his aid?

She did jump. She jumped up and away from the desk.

His face turned pale and he slid off his chair onto the floor.

Now what?

She wasn't sure what to do except sit back down and wait to make sure it was a done deal, that he was indeed dead.

She took a sip of her own coffee. It *was* good. She raised her cup in a toast to the empty seat across The Captain's desk. "Here's to a good day and many more of them."

37

Scotia and Ted finally arrived at The Cell.

"We're here," said Ted, slightly out of breath, "Now what? What's the big plan?"

"I'm going to see if they'll accept a bribe." She knew it wasn't a good plan. She didn't have a lot of money but it was something. If that didn't work, there was a good chance she'd be taken into custody, be given a sentence for trying to bribe a guard.

"Tell me you're joking."

"I'm not. But if they won't take the money, they'll probably take me. In which case," she smiled sarcastically at Ted. "It's best you head out now. I don't want you to get involved any more than you already are."

"I can't let you do this alone."

"You have to. I care about you. I don't want anything to happen to you, Teddy." Scotia kissed him on the lips.

"Wow. That's something I wasn't expecting."

"I know. Now leave."

"No. I want to help. Please let me. We need to be together no matter what happens."

She kissed him again, this time, more passionately, feeling something she'd never felt before. Her legs trembled, butterflies danced in her stomach.

❀ ❀ ❀

Brie had never been so scared in her life. Mary hadn't stopped crying since the guards had grabbed them from their room. Brie had checked out the area they were in several times but there wasn't really any place to run to. Even if she ran, she had no idea where to go. She also knew there was a good chance that once Scotia discovered what had happened, she'd never stop looking for her. She didn't want to get her sister involved any more than she already was. She wanted her to stay alive.

All of this was happening because Brie didn't know when to keep her mouth shut. She wished she could take it back but wishing wouldn't change a thing. She had to stop this line of thinking. It wouldn't help her. She had to figure something out.

"What are we doing here?" Mary asked between sobs.

"Yes. What are you going to do to us?" Brie pleaded.

"Welcome to The Calling."

❀ ❀ ❀

Kep heard it again. No, it wasn't his imagination. Some lunatic was banging on the door. All the guards had to do was scan their thumb and they'd be in. The Captain could access The Cell at all hours but he wouldn't be visiting this late and he always called ahead. Kep opened the door cautiously.

A male and female were standing there.

"Do you realize where you are?"

"Um, yes. I need a favor."

If they were waiting for him to invite them in, they were going to be waiting a long time. "Yeah?"

"I need to see my sister. Brie. It's an emergency. I can pay you."

Kep laughed and took a step back. This had to be a joke. One of the other guards had set him up. That had to be it. He laughed again.

"I'm serious. I'm Scotia and my sister's name is Brie."

Kep watched as the woman brought out a fat wad of cash from the front pocket of her jeans. Something was bugging him. The name was familiar. It would come to him in moment. "Do you know how much trouble you're in?"

"Yes, but she means the world to me and I'm willing to risk it."

Kep stared at the cash, wondering if there were some way he could allow this. Oh. Now it was coming back, A woman named Brie had arrived a few weeks earlier. She'd sparked his interest but there'd been drama around her so he'd thought it best to distance himself from her. Looks like he'd made the right call? "Give me a second."

He went around the corner to call Badger, the only one he could trust. And he'd give him a cut that would buy his silence for sure. "Badger. I have a proposition. Details later. Can you bring Brie to the lobby for a few minutes?"

❖ ❖ ❖

"You can't be serious," came Kep's voice from around the corner. A long pause then, "Damn. Okay."

Scotia had heard enough and it didn't sound good. She was done playing nice. She was running out of time.

"I need to see my sister."

"It's too late for her."

"Where is she?"

Kep's eyes remained focused on the floor.

Scotia clamped her hands over her mouth to stop herself from screaming. "It's The Calling, isn't it?"

"I'm sorry."

She had no plan but she started running.

Ted was right behind her.

Kep wasn't far behind.

38

Bev couldn't stand it any longer. She went around the desk to feel The Captain's neck for a pulse. She checked in three places to be sure. He was gone. His reign was over. No one would ever have to answer to him again. She hoped this was the beginning of something better.

At her office, she put together a few supplies: painkillers, gauze, bandages, and a few other nurse-like things so the guards wouldn't get suspicious and would let her into The Basement. She also grabbed a bottle of brandy and mixed crushed painkillers into it, hoping she might be able to disable a guard.

The plan was to get Valter out of there, make a run for it, then lie low until the chaos died down. She and Valter would be free to start their new life together. Was it foolproof? Not really. There was maybe a fifty-fifty chance of pulling it off.

Scotia heard a loud thud and turned around. Ted had taken Kep down. He was knocked out. Ted was staring down at him in shock.

"Let's go," urged Scotia. "We need to find out where The Calling takes place. That has to be where Brie is. We need to be quiet."

"Wait. I have an idea." Ted started tugging off Kep's uniform.

"What the heck are you doing? We don't have time for this."

"I'll put this on. I'll pretend I'm new. We're about the same size. They'll think I'm one of them and we'll get information. There's no way we can walk around the way we are."

"Good point. Hurry up."

"You can pretend you're one of my borders."

"Fantastic idea."

Moments later, Ted looked exactly like one of The Captain's guards, so much so, it was scary for Scotia as she put her arms behind her back to let him march her through the prison.

As they turned into another corridor, they met a woman in a nurse's uniform. Scotia wouldn't have thought The Captain would be interested in healing anyone in this section. The nurse seemed surprised to see them, too. "I don't think we've met. I'm Bev. The nurse here."

"I'm escorting this one for The Calling. Do you know where I'm supposed to go?" Scotia knew that Ted was wanting to appear confident but knew he was about to fall apart.

"I was asked to go to The Basement to treat a few of the borders. Do you know where that is?"

They were busted.

Silence, then it was Bev who spoke first. "Tell me who you are now or else I'll be making a call."

Scotia couldn't help it. "I'm looking for my sister. I was told she was taken for The Calling. You need to help me save her. I'm begging you."

39

Brie sat. She couldn't believe all the food. Of course she was hungry. She wanted to dive right in but she wouldn't let herself. Mary hesitated for only a second before she started eating. Then Brie couldn't resist any longer. She ate slowly, though. She didn't want the food to come back up. She had no idea what was going to happen next, but no matter what, there was one thing she knew for sure: she would need her strength. The tears came when she realized this was probably going to be her last meal. That she'd never get to say goodbye to Scotia.

Bev suggested that Ted would let the guards believe he was escorting Scotia to The Basement. She would tell them that The Captain had initiated a new rule whereby a nurse would be doing rounds and checking on the borders in The Basement.

With confidence, she addressed the first guard. "Spry, Captain Neal wants me to do a once-over on everyone. He also said he wanted to see you in his office to go over new rules or something."

"On my way."

Bev flashed a sweet smile for Anton, too. "Captain sent down a drink for you. I'll pour it for you in a second."

"That's the one thing about The Captain. He's always willing to share."

Bev made a motion to Ted. He moved Scotia down the hall.

"Hey, what's going on?" said Anton.

Ted replied. "This one spit on The Captain. Got thirty days."

"Carry on then." As Bev predicted, guards were more interested in their drinks than in what took place in The Basement.

She quickly poured and handed the glass to Anton, hoping that Scotia and Ted would locate Valter. Nobody within her eyesight was acting any differently. This was good but she had to make sure Anton was out before making any moves.

❊ ❊ ❊

Spry knocked on The Captain's door twice then waited, wondering what he should do. He could leave and track down The Captain later, or he could try the door to see if it was unlocked. The knob turned so it was. If The Captain wasn't in the office, he could use that as his defense if questioned later. He didn't want to take the chance that The Captain was here and too focused on paperwork to hear him knocking.

He pushed and the door opened to reveal the office cloaked in darkness. He switched the light on to see The Captain sprawled out on the floor. He ran over quickly to check him. *No pulse. Nothing. What has happened? Whatever it is, I'm too late.*

At first paralyzed with fear, he thought of calling for backup, but he didn't. *Think, Spry. Think.* He never did like The Captain. He'd only agreed to do the things asked of him because he wanted to survive. The Captain was evil, going too far with his rules. Maybe he could somehow use this death to his advantage. He could come up with something. If he needed more time, he'd call Anton, tell him The Captain was keeping him longer than he'd expected.

He locked the office door from the inside, turned off the main light, and sat on the chair. To anyone passing by, it would look as though The Captain had left for the evening.

Brie had been eating but whispered to Mary to eat more slowly. She was sure that as soon as they were done, The Calling would be next and then it would all be over. She had no idea how much longer she could stall. She needed a plan but her mind was blank. If she made a run for it, one of the guards would probably shoot her. It wasn't worth the risk. She wanted to find out what kind of game The Calling could be. She needed an advantage, anything.

"It's time." A guard appeared beside them and grabbed their wrists.

This got Mary sobbing again. "No!"

The moment Brie felt that grip on her wrist, her heart sank. It was over. There was no way out now. She was dragged away and chained.

After sitting there for mere minutes, Spry knew it was best to leave The Captain's office. He hadn't been able to come up with a believable explanation if he were caught in there with the dead Captain. He'd be charged with murder and the punishment would be death. He left The Captain undisturbed, closed the door to the office and left.

✾ ✾ ✾

Badger couldn't remember the last time he'd had a good night's sleep.

These Callings were taking their toll. Everything was getting out of hand and they were happening all the time now. He didn't want to go against The Captain, but he couldn't keep following his orders. There had just been a Calling and now another one was scheduled for tonight.

Tonight's Calling wasn't just a regular one, either. It was the one in which that girl, Brie, would be participating. She was someone his cousin Ted knew, and Badger had seen her a few times around the prison. There was something special about her. It wasn't that he was attracted to her, it seemed more personal than that.

Badger checked his watch for messages. The Calling should have started twenty minutes earlier but The Captain hadn't called. He always called to tell Badger to go take the bets. Very strange. Badger called The Captain's office. No answer. Something was wrong.

He headed out.

✿ ✿ ✿

Finally, thought Bev. *Anton's out like a light.* For how long, she had no idea but she headed in the same direction Ted had taken Scotia and she found them sitting beside Valter.

Bev wrapped her arms around Valter. "Are you okay?"

"I am now that you're here. Why *are* you here?"

"We have to get out of here fast."

"I need you to bring another guy, too. Amos." Valter pointed in the direction that Amos's voice had always come from.

Scotia said, "Do you know where they take people for The Calling?"

"It would've already started," said Bev. "But we may still have time. Valter, Amos, grab everyone who's able to walk and make your way to the section that's still under construction. The place they call Rain. Go, I'll meet you there. Anyone who's sick, tell them we'll come back for them."

Bev grabbed Scotia's hand, Scotia grabbed Ted's, and Bev led them—running—toward the barn.

41

Badger knocked on The Captain's door. No answer. Without hesitation, he checked the doorknob, surprised it was unlocked. He opened the door and turned on the light to see The Captain on the floor. He quickly ran over to realize the man was gone. Instinct told him this was a good thing. Perhaps the city could start over again. Without hesitation, he turned off the light, shut the door and ran toward the barn. Maybe it wasn't too late. Maybe he could stop The Calling. They may or may not have started without him. Who knew what the guards had been instructed to do?

As they approached the barn, Bev heard sobbing. "Oh, no," she whispered.

"I hear someone over there," said Ted. "We better get inside quick."

"Let me do the talking," Bev whispered. "I'm the nurse so I can talk my way out of this." She opened the door of the barn.

Brie was there. Scotia saw her and ran, wrapping her in her arms but Brie didn't move. "Don't worry we're going to get you of here."

Within seconds, several guards had entered. "What are you doing here," said one of them. It was Blake. "The Calling hasn't even started.

When it's over, we'll call you." He raised his wrist to make a call on his watch. "What's everyone doing here? What's going on?"

Bev reached out to move Blake's arm down. "I wouldn't do that if I were you."

Ted stepped in. "Hand over the key for the shackles. Now."

Bev's eyes never left Blake's as he handed the keys over. Ted gave them to Scotia who unlocked, first Brie, then Mary.

Bev turned in time to see Badger run in. Out of breath, he approached her. She decided she'd wait for him to speak first. She had no idea what his intentions were.

"All Callings have been canceled until further notice," Badger told Blake. Blake glared at Badger, then at Bev.

"Where's The Captain," Blake demanded. "Why isn't he here?"

"Everyone is to go home," Bev said, guiding people toward, then out, the door. "The Captain is calling an emergency meeting in town for tomorrow. He's preparing for it now."

❀ ❀ ❀

Valter was in good shape and Amos wasn't too bad, all things considered. They checked a few of the others and there were only three unable to move on their own. Together, Valter and Amos were able to evacuate everyone except for the guard and the three borders who couldn't move.

When everyone was safely relocated, people began asking questions. Everyone wanted to know what had happened to The Captain. They wanted to know if they were safe, what was going to happen next. Valter told them he didn't have any definite answers but assured everyone that in time, the answers would come. For now, they needed to rest because they'd no doubt need their energy over the next few days.

❀ ❀ ❀

Bev talked things over with Badger. He told her that The Captain was really ill. She let him go on for a bit before she jumped in to see what it was that Badger was really up to.

"If The Captain is so sick, I, as a nurse, should probably go see him, shouldn't I?"

"Um… Wait. He just needs his rest."

"I'm sure he won't mind. Maybe I can give him something to make him more comfortable."

Badger stared at her. "Is there something you're not telling me?"

"Perhaps there's something you're not telling *me*."

Badger stood silent for a moment. "You said The Captain mentioned having a town meeting tomorrow at noon."

"I did. Any idea why would he do that?" She was fishing.

"Maybe he wants to make some changes?"

They were on the same page. "What will be done with the guards who may not agree with these 'changes'?" *I can't go around poisoning* everyone. *It would be only a matter of time before I got caught. I don't dare push my luck.*

"Some will be transferred to another city and some will remain. I'm sure people won't care if The Captain's 'sick' for a while." Now it was Badger's turn to wiggle his eyebrows at her.

Bev couldn't help but laugh.

Badger smiled. "Blake and Spry may have to be transferred. Maybe Anton as well."

"Good to know."

❀ ❀ ❀

Finally it was time. Things were going to change. The first two doors that Bev opened, the rooms were empty. The third door, though, that's where everyone from The Basement was hiding. And there he was, her soulmate, Valter.

"I love you," Valter said as he wrapped both arms around Bev and lifted her up off her feet.

"I love you more."

About the Author

Catina Noble is a Canadian multi-genre writer. Her work is eclectic and provides something for everyone. She has over two hundred publications including her books, short-stories, poetry and articles. Her work has appeared in several publications, including, but not limited to: *Chicken Soup for the Soul: Your 10 Keys to Happiness, Woman's World Magazine, Bywords Magazine, Y Travel Blog, Canadian Newcomer Magazine, The Prairie Journal, The Mindfulword, Perceptive Travel* and many others. In 2013, her poem, "You Can't See Me," won first place in the Canadian Author's Association (NCR) poetry contest. Four of her books *Finding Evie, Vacancy at the Food Court & Other Short Stories, I'm Glad I Didn't Kill Myself*, and *Everest Base Camp:*

Close Call have won the Reader's Favorite silver seal of approval. She has a B.A. in Psychology from Carleton University, Social Services Worker Diploma from Algonquin College and is a recent graduate of the Creative Writing Program at Algonquin College. She currently writes, works full time in her field, and is enrolled in the Addictions & Mental Health Program at Algonquin College Her favorite place to write is at a local coffee shop.

To read more about her work, visit Catina's webpage at Crowe Creations, http://crowecreations.ca/catina-noble.html.